COUNTDOWN TO DESTINY

DARA GROWESOM

Contents

1

CHAPTER 1

Arizona just doesn't get it, this big hype about Valentine's Day. She doesn't get the cute, frilly cards or the roses, and she definitely doesn't understand the chocolates. Like, oh fun! Now instead of stuffing square-shaped chocolates down her throat, her diabetes will come in the form of heart-shaped chocolates instead!

"Duuuude."

"This is freaking adorable, oh, my gosh!"

Is it bad to say that at this point, all her friends' faces and names just blur together?

"Arizona?" Whom Arizona now affirms is Gem leans her head down the tiniest inch to get Arizona to meet eyes with her. She doesn't, just follows the sentence onto the next page of her book. Taking a bite of the squishy pear in her hand, she hums absent-mindedly. Before Arizona can blink, the fruit is snatched out of her hand and, much to her distress, tossed expertly into the trashcan a few meters away from where she sits with her so-called friends. Thing is, friends usually don't throw away other friends' foods. She sighs and slumps in her seat, pouting at Gem half-heartedly.

"That was my pear," she whines to her, the which the response is a simple roll of her eyes.

"What are you doing for Hearts Day?" Romy asks Arizona eagerly. She has this habit of calling holidays by their symbol's name, which Arizona thinks is totally ridiculous. Like, Valentine's is Hearts Day, Halloween is Pumpkin Day, Thanksgiving, Turkey Day.

"Eating," she answers, distracted again by the book before her. "TV."

"You're eating television?" Crosley asks with what he believes is dry humor from across the table and Arizona meets his eyes briefly to shoot him an unamused look. He thinks he's funny, but he really actually isn't.

"Oh, haha. Such great humor," she rolls her eyes before ducking down again. At this rate, finishing the book by the Friday will be impossible. At this rate, finishing the book by Friday will be impossible. See, Arizona has this horrid habit of reading every book within two days, except for those required for class. Reading Heart of Darkness is the last thing she wants to do right now, but it serves as a good excuse for not participating in ridiculous conversations like the one people are trying to get her to take part in right now. She sees Crosley stick his tongue out from the corner of her eye before grinning and leaning over to flick her on the cheeck. Arizona whacks his hand away irritably and glares. He shoots her a look, and sighing, Arizona shuts the hardcover shut.

"You guys do understand there is still more than one month left until Valentine's Day, right?" she questions with raised eyebrows and Romy snickers.

"And that's why it's just so sweet that he asked her out now." Romy also has a habit of having to stress at least one word in every sentence she says.

"Who's he?" Arizona gives Gem a blank look, who sighs as if she is a hopeless case—which she knows Arizona is definitely not.

"Rick."

"Rick?" Her eyebrows rise in surprise. "Rick the Dick?" Some new girl at their school had dubbed him that and turns out that it was quite catcy, so it had made it's way to almost everybody's vocabulary.

"That's the one," Crosley mumbles around his dinner roll just as Gem snaps at Arizona for not to call him that.

"Huh," Arizona paints an eh face on and shrugs when Gem gives her a questioning glance. "I just thought that Crosley would ask you." At the mention of his name, a light pink color tinges his cheeks and Arizona bites back a grin. Gem, on the other hand, can't control the full-out blush spreading across his face.

"There's nothing going on between us," she mutters, eyes downcast, and with a nudge to Arizona's side, Romy wiggles her eyebrows at our other two friends.

"Please," Romy sighs. "The sexual tension between you two is thick enough to slice with a butter knife." Arizona grins and nods whole-heartedly, the only response they receive being the bird from Crosley.

He and Gem aren't like all those other best friends who are hopelessly in love, but are just too naïve to realize. No, they know what is between them, but they are just too much of cowards to face it. It's depressing and half the reaspon for why Arizona has stopped caring about valentines. The other half is that she had to adapt, seeing as she has never had one in her entire life.

"Okay, that is so not true," Gem protests while Crosley stuffs his mouth with pasta so he doesn't have to say anything for a while.

"It is, though," Romy counters aptly, just as Briana plops down on the other side of Crosley.

"It really is," Briana agrees, as if knowing exactly what we're talking about. After delicately folding one of Crosley's noodles into her mouth, she turns to look at each of the group expectantly in turn, as if to ask what exactly they are talking about. Arizona leans over to whisper in her ear what they had been discussing prior to her arrival. With a knowing smirk, she straightens up. "MY first statement still stands," she informs the flustered pair. "It really is true."

"It's not!"

"Shut up, Crosley, you're weird and nobody likes you."

"Except Gem."

"Fuck you."

The rain sings a steady patter against the window. Today it sounds like screaming, but most probably only because she is screaming on the inside, when she thinks of what is waiting for her at home. Or, who is waiting for her at home.

She had decided to come to The Number, the neighborhood restaurant-café, after school to finish her homework. Lara is supposed to come home for a visit of a month, and rumor has it that she is dragging her new boyfriend along, as well. The last thing Arizona wants to do is meet her perfect older sister with her perfect grades and her perfect voice and her perfect boyfriend. Her mom and dad are expecting her, but a part of Arizona knows that they'll be partially glad that they'll have at least two extra hours before the yelling ensues.

Now, the book lays open before her, spine-up, as she rests her head on her arms crossed on the marble table. Tilting her head slightly, Arizona's eyes follow water droplets sliding down the glass, like a sledding race.

"Do you, uh. Do you want a refill? For your coffee?" a hesitant voice asks from behind Arizona and slowly, she twists her head back around to meet eyes with a pair of light blue ones. She smiles at the girl and slides the mug over to the edge of the table for her to fill to the brim with coffee again. The restaurant is family-owned, so all the workers look pretty much the same: pretty, dark-haired, either blue or brown eyes. This one is one of the younger twin sisters.

"Thanks," Arizona tells her when she's done and with a shy smile, she hurries back to the back room again. Cute.

It's probably been a couple hours and her parents are probably getting worried, so sighing, Arizona chugs down the coffee as fast as possible without burning her tongue, places it into the dirty dish bin in the corner of the room, and exits the glass door. The wind outside is cold and nips at her bare ears, forcing her to pull her hood further down her forehead, nearly blocking her sight.

Arizona's house is lit up unnaturally when she reaches it and stepping over the threshold, she can hear happy voices filtering into the dark hall. She tries to shut the door silently, but her mom with her super hearing catches it and calls out.

"Arizona, that you? Your sister's here!"

Oh, joy.

"Mhm," the girl hum back, flipping her hood off. She walks into the dining room as slow as she can. Arizona's sister's back is towards her and so is a new one she has never seen before. Lara turns in her seat when she hears Arizona.

"Zona!" she cringes at the name the older girl had given her and shoots Lara a smile which is more a grimace than anything.

"Lara," Arizona responds with half as much enthusiasm. Not that her sister is actually happy to see her. Bullshitting is Lara's talent. She has bullshitted her way through her entire life. Arizona only nods at the boy sitting next to her sister, because God knows that trying to remember the name of this human being that she will most probably never see for the rest of her life, will be a perfect waste of energy she can spend online. Every time she comes, Arizona's older sister comes with her latest boy-toy. She goes through the opposite gender like Arizona does books and fruit snacks. Arizona has an interesting obsession over fruit snacks.

Of course, her parents arere totally okay with this since it means Lara is pretty and smart and everything every single fucking boy out there looked for. Arizona used to get mad about that, seeing as she's never even been kissed before (if you didn't count that one time with Crosley when she was four) and there's basically next to no chance of her getting a boyfriend in the next decade.

"I'm Ross," the man offers now, and Arizona blinks at him before smiling back slightly.

"Arizona."

This time, Lara has gone for the All-American type: dark blonde hair, blue eyes, light-wash jeans.

"How long have you been together?" Arizona smile at the two innocently, taking her spot in the chair by her father, though her insides are still screaming. They tend to do that a lot when Lara is around. They don't scream for anything, really. They just make a lot of imaginary noise that Arizona finds amusement in. She likes to imagine that her insides screaming is symbolic, but it's probably just their natural reaction to Lara the she-demon.

Soon, food is piled on the plate to Arizona's chin and she returns to staring at them expectantly. "Nine months," Lara says proudly and Arizona nearly chokes. If Ross and Lara had sex without protection the first day they met, Arizona could be an aunt right now, as they speak. Weird.

"Nine months?"

They nod, Ross looking slightly confused.

"Jesus, congratulations, Lara! That's a milestone for you," she grins at her older sister, who shoots her a pointed glare. Arizona's mouth just widens. She is not always like this, really. Just in front of Lara.

"Zona, now is not the time, hon'," Mom reprimands from the other side of the table.

"That's not my name, Mom."

She just hums in response, then returns to firing questions at poor Ross. He seems like a nice guy, despite Arizona's earlier actions towards him. She decides he's okay, and besides, there is always this part of her that respects every one of Lara's boyfriends a whole lot, because, they have enough willpower to not punch their girlfriend's face into the nearest wall.

Then again, Lara is very pretty: maybe, that's what stops them. She is Arizona's half-sister. She's half Japanese, half Bengali, which Arizona thinks is totally, totally unfair, because that means Lara has a creamy, caramel complexion and eyes so dark that they're almost black, and Arizona has always wanted dark eyes. What's even more unfair, is that she looks basically nothing like her older sister. Lara's mother had died in a car accident when she was three, and her dad, Ben, had married Arizona's divorced mother, Cora: a thin, pale blonde, when Lara was four. Arizona had been born the same year. As it happens, she came out with more of Cora's features, but somehow, she had gotten her father's eyes, so she was so very, very blond, but with almond eyes, which really is an unnatural combination. Cora loves it and Arizona doesn't hate it, necessarily. She just thinks it's super weird. The first time she met Crosley, he had said that he didn't understand her face. She has learned, since then, not to take comments like that personally.

"So, Zona, honey." She knows that tone. The tone her mother uses for boys and the tone that makes her dad slightly uncomfortable. "Ross, here, says that he has a very single younger brother just a year older than you!"

"Really." Arizona pokes the hummus on the plate with her bread. It looks funny.

"Yes. And I was thinking that since you don't—"

"No, Mom," she interrupts what everybody at the table (except, maybe, Ross) knows will be a spiel on how Arizona would go yet another year without a boy, because, you know, that's the only thing that will ever make any girl happy. To be quite honest, Arizona's not that one person who gets mad from just the mention of boys being better than girls at something (this includes height)—that job goes to Romy—but, somehow, Arizona's mother's proximity always seems to bring it out of her. "Don't need no boy to be happy, Ma."

Her dad grunts but she is pretty sure that he's only agreeing because he had gone through quite the process when Lara had pranced home with her first boyfriend in the seventh grade. After the fifth one he gave up, knowing that she would be the one breaking the hearts.

"Double negative," says Lara, which Arizona chooses to ignore.

"I'm not saying that, honey," Cora smiles with pursed lips, white-blonde hairs falling out of her low ponytail to frame her thin face. "All I'm saying is that you're going to college in just a few months, and I think it'd be great for you to experience some, uh," her eyes flick to Lara for help, who nods encouragingly, "experience some of the outside world."

Arizona sighs heavily, setting her fork down with a clatter. "See, that's the thing, Mom. College is where you "experience the real world." And keeping relations with a boy back here when I go to New York? Yeah, don't think that's a wonderful idea."

"But—"

"Mom. I'll meet someone next year, probably. God, give it a rest, will you? Jesus."

"I'm just worried that it won't happen to you, though."

Ben covers Cora's hand soothingly, and Arizona snorts. The amount of faith her mother has in her and her love life is quite astonishing. Quickly, she shoves the rest of the potatoes into her mouth and stands up abruptly, dish in hand. "'Kay, bye. Swell to have you back, Lara," she grins over-enthusiastically at her sister, then leaves to place the plate and utensils in the kitchen sink. Her family has never been very proper, and never in her life has she ever been asked to be excused from—well, anywhere, really. That's probably one of the things she truly loves about her household.

She chugs down a glass of water, sets it down on the counter, and runs past the dining room and down to the basement, to her room. Arizona also loves the fact that her room is all the way in the last floor, away from everybody else's situated at the top floor. It gives her privacy and the right to blast music at any time of the day (or night). Also, she can sing in the shower without embarrassing herself, which is a major plus.

Arizona's favorite spot in the entire world is her room. The walls are plain, but nobody can tell because of the books. She has books everywhere. Everywhere. They're stacked under her windows, on the windows, by the bed, under it, lining the walls. Over time, her room has developed a kind of old bookstore smell, and it's probably the best thing ever. Arizona had started working in freshman year just to afford all the books she wanted, but just as college got scarily close, she was fired. To this day, she still isn't certain just why she was, but as far as she's concerned, her old boss, Clint at Wal-Mart, could go fuck himself.

Now, Arizona picks up her notebook and pen from where they lay on her bed and sets the paper on her lap, pen hovering over it. She has always wanted to write, but just can never find the right words to start the story off with. She's heard that some other girl at her school got her book published and thinks that that must be the coolest feeling in the world, and has decided that it doesn't hurt to try. Personally, Arizona believes she is better at reading than writing, but maybe she isn't total shit at the writing part (though she is ninety-nine percent sure that she is). So far, she has one sentence written, and absolutely no clue where to go with it.

The first things Eden noticed the moment she stepped out of her rusty, blue Chevrolet was that it was hot and that it was crowded.

After about half an hour of staring at the words she had written, like last week, and tapping her pen to the beat of the radio, Arizona sighs and throws it onto the bed. And then, she decides that she is one hundred percent sure that she is better at reading than writing, which she is total shit at.

2

CHAPTER 2

Arizona loves school. No one she has ever told that to, thinks she is sane. But she does. She does love it. She loves how she gets to see her friends for seven hours straight. She loves how photography and film is a class and she gets graded on pictures she takes. She loves how they have an entire hour of study hall where reading for the first half is a must. She loves how teachers love the fact that she reads. But, most of all, she loves how at school, she gets seven sure hours away from Lara May.

Her older sister has been here for nearly an entire month, and apparently Arizona had been wrong—Lara is staying for even longer. Now, she slams her bag down very agressively next to her stool before sliding in. She likes Bio because the teacher is probably the best ever and doesn't care if she reads in class, as long as she maintains an A in the class. And really, isn't that all school is about? Keeping a good grade point average so your parents don't yell at you and you get fed properly every night? (Once, Arizona had gotten a C in seventh grade and her parents had refused to feed her. No wifi is one thing, but really? No fruit snacks?)

In angry, jerky movements, Arizona pulls out her current book, slamming it open on the yellow table. It's a collection of short stories from The New Yorker she had found lying around at work. Just as she begins reading, someone else slips into the seat across from her, on the other side of the elevated table. Arizona's eyes flit up to meet those of Jeremy Miller's, and she smiles.

Jeremy Miller is nice. He's one of those kids you see around school and in class and you say hi or you smile or something and that's that. He's one of those kids that you're friendly with, but not necessarily friends, so you call him by both his first and his last name. He's Arizona's Bio lab partner and she can't really complain, because he never, ever procrastinates and isn't a total douchebag—which basically almost all of the straight male population of Washington High is.

"Hey, Arizona," he smiles at her. Oh, and one more thing: Jeremy Miller is cute, with his dark, dark hair and warm, brown eyes, but his smile is killer. Like, it's actually so gorgeous and Arizona has no idea how that even works.

"Hey, Jeremy," she says back, shooting him a fleeting smile as he pulls out the worksheet that—damn it. "Oh, shit, I totally forgot to do that!" her eyes widen. The thing about Mr. Han, the Bio teacher, is that he may be totally fine with her reading in class, but he is terrifying when you don't turn in your work on time. Rapidly, she scrambles to fill in the answers. "Can I, uh, do you—um, have prob—"

"Here," Jeremy Miller grins his killer grin, pushing his own work-sheet towards her. Arizona nearly cries from relief.

"Oh, my god, thank you, Iloveyousomuchloweyouforevery-ou'rethebest." Taking it, she copies the answers down quickly and hands the paper back to the amused boy. When happy or relieved,

Arizona has a habit of slurring her words together. "Seriously, thank you."

"It's no problem," he shrugs, still smiling. It's killing Arizona.

When Mr. Han calls for the class' attention, she sighs and faces the front, chin in hand. "Make sure to wash your hands, 'kay? Awesome, I need two people to help pass the frogs out." What? Arizona's head snaps up and she spots the little bins with frogs on them coming towards her. Their stomach's face up and she groans, head falling down ontot he table.

"Ugh, I forgot about the dissection."

"Yeah?" Jeremy Miller smiles a half smile and she nods, pursing her lips. It's not that Arizona doesn't like dissections, she does, but the last time she has dissected a frog, it had been in seventh grade and all she remembers is the distinct horrendous small that had overtook the room. Jeremy Miller hands her a pair of vinyl gloves, which she snaps on and watches as he does the same. He brushes his black hair out of his eyes and reaches for the exacto knive-looking thing. Arizona decides to be helpful and read out the directions for him to follow, which he does very carefully.

Jeremy Miller slowly cuts one, straight line down the abdomen and then two small ones pulled out from the center, so the two have a wonderful view of the reptile's innards. Arizona leans over to peek in before drawing back with a gag. The frog has eggs in its stomach.

"Holy fucking shit," she cries, hunching over, away from the table and Jeremy Miller's eyebrows rise as he watches her with a touch of concern shadowing his face.

"You okay?" he asks.

"No," Arizona shakes her head rapidly. "No, it has eggs in its stomach. Too much, too much."

She actually has no idea why the eggs are affecting her so badly.

"Do you have trypophobia, or something?"

"What the hell is that?" she makes a face, not being able to unsee the image.

"Fear of, like, a lot of circles."

"Yeah, I guess so," Arizona blows her cheeks up with air, letting it all go with a whoosh. Her head is ringing and she is almost certain that she is going mad.

"Here, water," he hands her a cup, from where, she has no idea, but she takes it gratefully. "You can just, uh, answer the questions, and I'll do the dissection."

"You are seriously the best human being ever, I would hug you if I weren't shivering all over because of the holephobia or whatever," she tries her best to smile and he laughs .

"I don't mind the shivering," he murmers, turning back to the frog, and Arizona blinks.

"What?"

"Nothing," he shakes his head with a small smile, and she peers at him curiously.

So, they work like that for some few moments, quiet, save for when Arizona asks for Jeremy Miller's help on some questions. Then,

"So, Valentine's Day's coming up," Jeremy Miller looks up at Arizona, who prior to the conversation, has been drawing something (she has no idea what) that resembles almost a dick, on the table. Immediately, she erases it quickly, and smiles at the boy.

"It is," her head bobs up and down in an uncertain way, and she clears her throat, looking anywhere but at the very pregnant frog. Why, though? Why would Mr. Han buy a pregnant frog for them to dissect?

"Got a hot date?" he asks and she snorts without meaning to.

"Yeah, you bet I do," Arizona smirks, rolling her eyes, and Jeremy Miller jerks up in surprise, an indistinguishable look on his face.

"Wait, seriously? You do?"

"No! 'Course not. Never have, never will," she laughs, scrunching her nose up in distaste.

"Sure you will," he grins at her and she shrugs.

"Probably not, but that's okay. I'm used to it after almost two decades of it."

Jeremy Miller laughs a small, breathy laugh and pushes the frog away, pulling his gloves off. He saunters to the sink, where he washes his hands and dries them with a rough, paper towel, wiping the rest of the water on his jeans.

"How about you?" she asks after he returns the bin with the disgustingly pregnant frog to table in the front.

"How about me what?"

"Do you have a valentine?" Arizona is really just trying to make dull conversation, but his answer piques her interest.

"I'm hoping to."

"Really? Who?" Arizona has never been like this with Jeremy Miller, before, but something about where this conversaion is headed makes her feel as if she has known the boy forever. Maybe because it's a conversation she would have with her girlfriends. Or Crosley, since he's basically one of the girls, which Arizona finds quite amusing.

"Uh, you," Jeremy Miller responds after a minute, clearing his throat uncertainly. Arizona blanches, blinking because she is near certain that she did not hear correctly. Maybe blasting music at all hours isn't such a great idea, anymore.

"I'm sorry?"

"You, Arizona. Do you, uh—do you want to, maybe, go out with me? On Valentine's Day?"

"Oh, um." She is stuttering. Arizona May is stuttering. She has always liked to think that she doesn't stutter, but now here she is; this cute boy with a killer smile is making her stutter. "Sure."

Sure? Sure? Arizona is not sure. Arizona is anything but sure. Now, she is beating herself up internally because her mouth has no idea how to work with her brain and it runs on its own, especially when she doesn't want it to, and now she has a date on Valentine's Day. It might as well be the apocalypse.

Crosley is poking Arizona's cheek with a celery stick and she doesn't even have enough drive to slap it away. "Hey, what's wrong with you?" he asks, peering at her curiously, and she looks up to meet his questioning gaze.

"Nothing. Get that vegetable away from me before I slam your head against the table," she mutters, eyes glazed as she stares at the book before her. It's not even open.

"What happened?" Romy decides to join in the prying and Arizona is so very close to throwing cafeteria trays at their faces because she is trying to think. Or, not think, in this case. She wishes that there is a delete button in her mind, which she can press and just erase the memories of the entire day from her brain's database.

"Uh," she clears her throat. "Jeremy Miller asmuhhhhh..." she mumbles into her shirt, ducking her head down. Crosley narrows his eyes and leans closer to her, and now Arizona has the rapt attention of the rest of the table. Fun.

"Say that again?" Gem says and Arizona sighs, sitting straighter.

"Jeremy Miller, um, asked me out. On Valentine's Day."

Immediately, Gem squeals loud enough to draw gazes from the next table over, and throws her arms around Arizona, squeezing the now-flushing girl to her bountiful chest. "My Ari is finally growing up! Finally! I'm so proud of you, oh, my god, finally!"

"You need to calm yourself," Crosley blinks at her before turning back to his best friend. "What did you say, then? Arizona?"

Uncertainly, she sucks her top lip into her mouth, biting it with her bottom teeth. "Uh...yes?"

"Whoa," Crosley sits back, eyebrows risen.

"What does that mean?" Arizona scowls at him, who only shrugs, now also smirking alongside Romy and Gem.

"I just never thought that'd happen to you. Not in high school, at least."

To be quite honest, Arizona hadn't thought so, either, but Crosley voicing his thoughts made her just the slightest bit offended. "Rude," she mutters, but he only grins, throwing an arm over her shoulders. Despite her prior comment, she burrows into his shoulder. "I'm so fucking fucked, holy shit, I don't know how to go on dates? How the fuck do you go to dates? So fucking fucked," she complains into his shirt and with a face of disgust, he slowly pries her away from him.

"Hey, can you not cry on me, please?" he twists his face up at her jokingly and rolling her eyes, Arizona smacks his head.

"That's your job, Crosley. I'm supposed to cry on you; that's what bee eff effs do."

"Then, in that case, Romy can be your bee eff eff. Have fun." He shoves Arizona at Romy, who yelps, nearly spilling her water over her vegetable burger.

"What the hell, dude?" Romy whines, shaking the water droplets off of her bare arms. "I almost got my burger soggy!"

"Oh, no, because the vegetable burger would taste so bad only after getting wet," Crosley mocks snarkily and Gem flicks his arm. Romy makes a face at him. She is a strict vegan, and has been since the eighth grade; something about her dad running over an already dead bird that had been lying in the middle of the road at night. Crosley, for some reason, has always felt antagonized because of Romy's habits; mostly because he loves meat so much. "Seriously, though," he makes a weird face. "A vegetable burger is, like, the biggest oxymoron, ever."

"That would actually be summer school," Briana looks up briefly from her sketchbook to grin at everyone. "Oh, and congrats, Zona."

"It's not a goddamn win, or something, could everyone please not congratulate me on getting a date, please?"

"You said please twice," Crosley points out and she shoves his head down, but he stops at the last moment, just above his salad, which happens to have a lot of dressing.

"You're going to be saying please way more than twice when I'm kicking your ass," Arizona retorts and sticks her tongue out, but Briana butts in, again.

"Actually, he's going to be saying please when Gem is doing other things to his ass."

Arizona spits out her water, Gem slams her fork down and stands up with a huff, Romy snorts loudly, and Crosley's face is golden. "What the fucking fuck is your fucking problem. I can't believe I'm friends with you dipshits. I can't believe it," he mutters, throwing lettuce at all of them. When Arizona looks up from the spill she has created on the table, Gem is gone. All the friends can do (except for

Crosley, who is scowling so hard that his face resembles something like a prune) is grin at each other.

3

CHAPTER 3

It's Valentine's Day, and apparently, Arizona has to actually pay attention to what she wears, because, this year, she has a valentine, as weird as that sounds. As of now, she has her head buried in the closet, all articles of clothing flying out onto the bed behind her, the rare hanger coming loose and hitting the walls.

When the knock sounds at her door, Arizona jumps and swivels on her heels to watch as Lara slips into the room, shutting the door behind her. "Happy Valentine's Day," she smiles uncertainly at Arizona, who frowns back, only slightly confused.

"Uh, yeah, sure. Why are you here, again?"

"C'mon, Zona, you have to get over your grudge or whatever at some point," Lara sighs, and scoffing, Arizona sits down on her bed, arms crossed over chest.

"I'm holding a grudge? Please, it's just because you think you're so much better than me," she rolls her eyes and follows the other girl as she walks across the room to the closet and starts sorting through Arizona's clothes. She doesn't care anymore. "It's because you think that you being prettier and smarter than me means that you've won at life. Well, guess what, Lara! Bullshit. 'Cause you're a bullshitter, and yeah, maybe you are prettier and smarter than me, but you also go through boys like crazy, I mean why? And what are you doing in the—"

"How about this?" Lara pulls out of the doors, holding up an assembly of a pair of loose, sunflower yellow, high-waisted shorts and a flowy, black t-shirt.

"What?" Arizona asks blankly. "What are you doing?"

"I'm figuring out your Valentine's Day outfit, duh," Lara makes big eyes at her and then shoves the clothes at Arizona. "That is what you were doing when I came in, right? Well, problem solved."

"See?" Arizona cries. "This is your problem! You think you're better than me at everything."

"What?" Lara blinks. "Just put the goddamn clothes on, Jesus." And then she turns and marches out of the door, closing the door. Arizona looks down at the clothing in her hands and huffing, takes her pajamas off. Might as well.

So, she tugs the shorts on over a pair of black tights, and then pulls the shirt over her head, tucking it into the pants, before slipping into a pair of flats. She grumbles because it looks pretty (correction: very) good together. "This is cute," Arizona mumbles.

"I know," comes Lara's voice from outside, and Arizona yelps in surprise.

"What the hell? Why are you still here?"

And then Lara enters the room again. A slow smile spreads over her delicate features.

"Perfect."

"Perfect," Arizona mocks in a falsetto voice, face screwed up, and Lara gives her an unimpressed look. "Whatever. I'm only wearing this 'cause I don't have time to pick out my own clothes."

"I know."

"I still don't like you, you know."

"I know."

"That's super annoying."

"I know."

"You suck."

"M'kay."

"Go to hell, Lara."

"See you there, Zona."

"Don't call me that."

"M'kay."

In Bio, Jeremy Miller sits down after Arizona, as per usual. Maybe, Arizona should stop adding his surname to his title, and just call him Jeremy, because that is usually how normal people refer to their normal valentines. It's so weird, hearing valentine and thinking, "Yeah, I actually do have one, this year." Maybe, this date thing will go better than she is expecting. Or, maybe, it's just a one-time thing and then they'll go back to being Arizona and Jeremy Miller, partners in Biology class.

"Hey," she says, smiling, because she has decided that the last thing she wants is to have an awkward date with Jeremy Mi—Jeremy. Just Jeremy. Oh, dear God, she might start calling him Just Jeremy, now.

Jeremy, Jeremy, Jeremy, Arizona chants to herself. She has to get this right. She can only imagine just how horrifying it would be if she called him by Jeremy Miller or Just Jeremy in a conversation.

"Hi," Jeremy grins his killer grin back. Arizona wishes that he would put it away, because she is one second away from dying early. "Happy Valentine's Day," he tells her and she nods back, lips pursed.

"Yep. So, um, you doing anything? Today?"

"Well," Jeremy raises an eyebrow, looking mildly amused, "I am going on a date with this girl."

"Oh, yeah?"

"Mhm."

Arizona is near certain that she is supposed to throw an equally flirty line back, but none come to her at this moment, because, well, she just isn't used to conversations like...this. So, instead, she clears her throat and decides to avoid any eye contact with Jeremy for the remainder of the period.

"Happy Hearts Day, bitchachos." A pink, plastic bag is thrown before everyone at the table. They look like party favors, stuffed with candies and tied off at the top with a twist-and-tie. With a face, Crosley picks his up with his pointer finger and thumb, holding it away from him as he surveys it suspiciously.

"I swear to god, Romy, if these are made of vegetables, we're not friends, anymore."

"Please, go fuck Gem, or something."

"Hey, can you guys not use me when insulting Crosley, please?" the girl in question grumbles, untying the bag.

"Thanks, Romy," Briana grins at her, being the only one the in the group who even begins to have manners. It's pretty hilarious, seeing as she happens to crack the most perverted jokes and is also the sweetest human being Arizona has ever come across.

"See?" Romy sniffs, "Briana's cool, Briana's my friend."

"Ew, get off me, freak," Briana makes a horrified face at the other girl and inches away, dragging her sketchbook with her. But, then, she scoots back to hug Romy. Arizona laughs and leans down to pick at her own bag. It finally comes undone and her hand reaches in, emerging again with a box of Sweethearts.

"Ugh, why is this such stereotypical candy, Mee," Crosley peeks over Arizona's shoulder to look through the bag's contents. "Pink lollypops? Red M&Ms? Candy hearts? Bullshit." Then, he proceeds to grab the bag and throw it to the other side of the table, where it slides and falls off the edge, onto the disgusting cafeteria floor. Gasping, Arizona stands up and scuttles to the other side, to see if she can salvage any of the candy, but to her dismay, only one Baby Bottle has survived. Growling, she stands up again and marches to Crosley, whose head she shoves to the side, resulting in him tipping over onto Gem. Briana snickers and Arizona punches his arm.

"Asshole. I fucking hate you. You suck," Arizona mumbles, moving around to sit next to Gem, instead of next to Crosley, where she had been sitting before he had decided to throw her candy like the fucktard he is. Then, she snatches his bag and stuffs it down her shirt so he can't get it. Sighing, Crosley flips her off and then stuffs his pizza into his giant gob. "Good. Go choke yourself with food. You won't be missed," she shoves her hair out of her eyes, doing her best to shoot a death glare at the smirking boy.

Romy sighs wistfully, a precious smile on her lips. "I love holidays."

Lara says that Arizona's school outfit is good enough for a date, and as much as she doesn't want to care what her older sister thinks, she does, so she keeps it on. Everybody, including her, knows that Lara is usually (always) right about things like this. You know, like fashion and boys and life. Lara is usually right about everything, goddamnit.

Sighing, Arizona pulls her hair up into a high ponytail and folds some money into her shorts' pockets along with her phone and earbuds. Jeremy had offered to pick her up, but instantly, she had refused, secretly terrified of what would happen of Jeremy did pick her up and Lara opened the door. Shivering, she jogs up the stairs to the main floor, where Ross sits on the living room couch, watching the sports channel. As Arizona walks by, he looks up, and smiles at her.

"Hey, Arizona," he greets. Much to Arizona's bewilderment, for the past month, he has been quite...awesome, for lack of better terms. Ross is definitely different from all of Lara's past boyfriends; for one, he actually says hi to Arizona—and he even calls her by her whole name. And he treats Lara well; Arizona wishes that she doesn't care much about that, but she really, actually does. "Got a date?" he raises his brows at her apparel and she strikes a pose, grinning.

"Yep."

"What's his name?"

Arizona can almost, almost start to see him as an older brotherly figure, which is quite weird.

"Jeremy Miller," the name slides off her tongue, because it is what she is used to—though just Jeremy is coming easier to her, now.

Ross hums, flicking his blonde hair out of his face, before shaking his head. "Nope, don' t know him." Apparently, Ross had also gone to Washington High and knows a lot of the current highschoolers through older siblings.

"Oh. Well, he's cute and nice, and I've never had a date before, so I'm terrified, but that's okay," Arizona tries smiling, but it comes out as more of a grimace. Ross shoots her a thumbs up, facing towards the television. A bulky guy kicks a soccer ball and runs across the field, before some other, much leaner guy steals it away from him with his heel, taking it back to the other goal. Ross groans, cursing, then turns back to Arizona.

"It'll be great. Just don't talk too much about yourself because that is hella annoying."

"M'kay."

Shrugging on her jacket, Arizona slips back into the flats from before, and leaves the house with a wave at Ross. She is supposed to meet Jeremy at the restaurant, some fancy place that she has only ever driven past before. From what she's seen, it's all dark lights and elegance. Arizona is to meet him at six, so she has to set out a half hour early to get there on time. Driving, it takes around ten minutes, but since Arizona has neither a car or a driver's license, she has gotten quite used to walking around everywhere.

She pulls the jacket's collars up higher to block the wind rushing around her face. Arizona doesn't understand why Valentine's Day is in February, one of the coldest months, because Valentine's Day seems like such a summer holiday, what with all the love and the dresses. It had snowed a few days ago, and currently, only a gray sludge remains on the sides of the road. It is still probably a few degrees under zero, judging from how freezing the air around her is, and she has a knack for falling over random objects, so it only makes sense that it is Arizona of all people, whose shoe comes into contact with black ice. She then flails her arms around in a mad attempt at keeping herself up and off the ground, but of course, it doesn't help. Never have flailing arms helped anyone balance. Finally, grabbing a nearby tree branch, Arizona manages to save herself.

As it happens, though, one can only save oneself from one thing at a time, and in Arizona's case, this is death; what she doesn't save herself from is embarrassment. Because, when she looks up, she has found that she is in front of the restaurant and that there is a car parked by the curb, and no other than Jeremy Miller is leaned against it, a very amused grin lining his lip. Grumbling, Arizona straightens up and dusts imaginary dirt off her clothes. Brushing a hand through her hair (only to get it stuck above her braid), she walks towards the boy with as much dignity she can muster.

"You could have helped instead of just standing around, you know," she mutters, but he only responds with a cheeky smile.

"You look nice," Jeremy says instead, and Arizona can't stop the blush rising to her cheeks.

"I wore the same thing to school."

"You looked nice at school, too."

"Why are you so sassy?"

"I'm not sassy," he pulls a dramatically appalled face, placing a hand against his chest. "You're sassy. Now be quiet and take my compliment." Jeremy opens the passenger's door for her to sit down, which she does, and he shuts it before walking around the car to the driver's seat.

"You're so different at school," Arizona states as he stretches the seat belt over himself.

"Yeah?"

"Yeah. I like this you better, just so you know," she informs him, and he grins.

"I'll keep that in mind."

As he turns the key in the ignition, Arizona's eyebrows furrow. "Hold on, where are we going? Aren't we already at the restaurant?"

The smirk reappears and Jeremy switches on the blinker, turning right. "You think I have that kind of money? I don't, if you were wondering," he adds as she opens her mouth. "We're going to a movie and the best burger place, ever." Arizona can't help but laugh, because Jeremy is definitely not what she had expected, nor are his actions. It's a good thing, she decides.

Jeremy takes her to the latest Disney film at the theater and Arizona realizes that she hasn't fucked everything up, yet. It's an amazing feeling. Then, as promised, they arrive at a small complex of bakeries and restaurants downtown, and Jeremy parks in a nearby parking lot before leading Arizona to a tiny, white building wedged between a noodles restaurant and a café. The Little Big Burger.

"Hey, I think I've been here," she says, looking up at the vertical, red sign.

"I'd hope so. They have the best food."

They do have the best food, as Arizona finds out after a half hour. The inside is small and cute, with little, white tables and a modern feel. The fries are heaven, she learns, after stuffing her face with them.

"Hey, wanna know something?" Jeremy asks, setting his burger down.

"Okay."

Carefully, Arizona watches as he clears his throat and scratches the back of his head, suddenly looking incredibly sheepish.

"I've liked you for a while," he blurts finally and Arizona blinks.

"What, like a week, a while?"

"No. Like, a few months, a while."

Arizona then chokes on her cake, hacking. When he reaches out to pat her back, she waves it away. He hands her a cup of water, which she downs to put out the fire in her burning throat. She has a déjà vu moment to that horrid dissection in class. "You what?" Arizona finally gasps, putting a napkin to her mouth as she continues to cough.

"Like, I mean," he stumbles over his words and only now does Arizona realize how intimidating her demanding words can be to the poor boy. "I mean, you're just...different, I guess." When she raises her eyebrows in a silent question at the terribly cliché line, he continues after a second of hesitation. "You're always reading a different book every week. And you always look so detached from everything else—in a good way, of course. But then, when people come talk to you, you somehow make it as if you're interested. Though, I can tell you're just pretending to. But they can't, and that's amazing to me."

Arizona hadn't understood half the things he said, but something about it still makes her stomach erupt with warmth, because, it meant that he had...he had actually paid attention to her. A boy other than Crosley had paid attention to her.

"Oh. Wow, I mean. Wow. Okay."

He laughs uncertainly. "Sorry, was that too much? I didn't mean to scare you or anything. I just, uh, god damn it, my brother said I should just tell you, so I did, and this is wonderful, really. Now, I've scared you and I was going to ask you to be my girlfriend, too, and I'm so delusional it's not even funny, for God's sa—"

"Sure," Arizona says suddenly, because no for fuck's sake, she is not fucking sure. This is the second time with the same boy that she has said she's "sure," when she's not. But now, she can't take her words back, so she swallows her apology down and waits.

"What?"

"I'll be your girlfriend. Jeremy."

"Oh," he blinks. "Oh. Um, cool."

Arizona laughs because he's so cute. But, then, he smiles and he's gorgeous, not cute, and she decides that maybe it's not such a bad decision to be his girlfriend. What could go wrong?

Funny, how whenever the protagonist says that in any and every book she has ever read, everything does. Every single fucking thing goes wrong.

4

CHAPTER 4

When Arizona's mother had heard that she got a boyfriend, first she had squealed like a twelve-year-old, then she had kissed Arizona's father, which had resulted in the loss of Arizona's appetite, and then she had walked all the way around the dining table to gather Arizona to her chest, kissing the top of her head.

"I am so proud of you, oh, my God, I can't believe this! Ben, can you believe it?" Arizona had no idea how to react to this, because a part of her had been offended, while the other had been trying to grasp the facts, itself. Her having a boyfriend was still a foreign concept.

And when Arizona's mother had heard that she was going to meet his family, she had absolutely flipped her shits. When she had gone downstairs to get a drink of water, she had overheard her parents muttering to each other in the living room. Arizona couldn't hear exactly what they said, but some of her mother's whispers had sounded suspiciously like, might not, alone forever, and Ben! which, to be honest, hadn't been much of a surprise for Arizona.

But after two weeks of being Jeremy's girlfriend, he had deemed it to be a perfect time for introducing her to his family. Arizona can't lie—the prospect of meeting his (big, from what he has said) family is daunting, but this is her first ever relationship and the last thing she wants to do is screw it up. So, now, here she is, on the phone with Briana, ten minutes before Jeremy is supposed to pick her up. Arizona is camped out in front of her house, on the deck, so that she can leave without her mother or—God forbid—Lara interfering.

"I'm terrified, Briana. What the hell do I do? What if they ask me what I want to major in? I don't know what I want to major in," she cries, pulling at the roots of her white-blond hair.

"Jesus, you need to calm down," another voice pipes up from somewhere in Briana's background, probably. Arizona narrows her eyes.

"Christine?"

Christine is Briana's girlfriend. She's in college, studying film, she has a slight Scottish accent even though she's Vietnamese because she had moved to Scotland when she was fourteen, she listens to "high-definition music," as she puts it, and she plays piano, which Briana says she finds quite endearing. Arizona's only met her four times in the entire year the two have been dating, but she's talked to her a whole lot over the phone.

"Yep," Christine says now from the other line. "Hey."

"Hi," Arizona blinks. "Briana, are you there?"

"Yeah. Just breathe and don't talk too much if you know that your digging yourself a grave. Be polite, answer questions with as much interest as you can—"

"And don't crack any dirty jokes," Christine juts in. "When Bri met my parents, she decided that it would be terribly appropriate to make inappropriate jokes. It wasn't. At least my parents have forgotten about that, though."

Arizona bites her lip nervously, nodding even though they can't see her. "Okay, sure, yeah. But what if I do s—" And then Jeremy's blue Toyota pulls up and she curses. "He's here."

"Okay, you just really need to breathe and think before you say anything. Keep that in mind and you'll be golden." She can hear the encouraging smile in Briana's voice.

"M'kay. Thanks, guys."

"I hope this guy's hot, for you to be worrying so much," Christine says and Arizona smiles at Jeremy when he steps out of the car.

"He's pretty cute, I dunno," she smirks and Jeremy, obviously hearing, raises his eyebrows in amusement. "But, thanks," she repeats. "I'm going now. Bye." Turning off the phone, Arizona slips it into her pocket and walks slowly towards the boy.

"Pretty cute?" he asks with a grin and she shrugs.

"Eh, you know. You're okay," she sighs jokingly and he laughs.

"I see. Who were you talking to?"

"Briana. She goes to our school."

He nods, opening the passenger's side door for her, something she has noticed that he always does, and then shuts it before getting into the driver's seat. "Yeah, I know her. I think we were partners for some Lit project at some point."

Arizona hums and taps her fingers on the handle in the side of the door. Though she feigns comfort, her heart is pounding so hard that it rattles her ribcage, and the palms of her hands are sweating buckets. Over and over again, she wipes them down her jeans, but the rough material does nothing to improve the circumstances. Jeremy notices and she watches from the corner of her eye as his eyebrows rise and his lips tilt up slightly. "Relax, my family isn't the most terrifying one in the world," he says and Arizona breathes out a shaky chuckle.

"This is the first time, so I don't think it matters how scary the family is. I'm pretty sure I'm gonna be scared no matter what," she points out, blinking rapidly. Arizona searches for something to focus on, and finally chooses on the music spilling out of the car's speakers. "Who's this?" she asks. Jeremy glances at her before smiling slightly and looking forward.

"It's by Walk The Moon. The song's called Quesadilla."

Weird name. Good song.

"Is it the radio?"

"Nah," he says, "I listen to mostly just CD's. My brother never listens to the radio stations and makes a lot of mixes. I guess it rubbed off on me."

"How many brothers do you have, again?" Arizona asks just for the sake of conversation. She doesn't think that she can stand any silence in this ridiculous state she is in.

"Just one. Older one—he's nineteen."

"And sisters? You have a lot, right?"

"Just three. An older one, who's engaged. Has been for a few months. She's not here, right now. And two fourteen-year-olds. They're twins. One's going through a gothic phase and the other's in the artistic phase, where she decides to try out anything remotely artistic." Jeremy smirks. "Like, drawing or painting or music or writing or poems. Lots and lots of poems. But don't let that scare you; I think they're just really scared of everyone, themselves. Especially Jane, the goth."

"Oh," Arizona purses her lips and the car pulls onto a driveway. The house before them is normal-sized, probably a little bigger than

Arizona's, and the bright headlights bounce off the garage, even though it's not completely dark out yet. Only after the boy gets out, does she follow, smoothing out her silk shirt, which is completely useless, seeing as that silk has a tendency to be smooth all the time. After a moment of fumbling with her garb, she looks up to meet Jeremy's warm eyes, and he puts his hand out for her to take, which she does. If he can feel just how sweaty her palms are, he doesn't show it. Arizona isn't quite comfortable with all this touching yet, but she decides that it is quite nice and she will no doubt get used to it at some point or another.

With his empty hand, Jeremy fishes out a set of keys from his red jacket's pocket and inserts it into the door's lock, twisting it. The door swings open when he pushes it, and with a look back at Arizona, he steps in, pulling her with him. At home, she usually takes her shoes off, but when she makes a move to do that, Jeremy waves it away, telling her it's fine if she keeps it on. He does, so she does, too.

"Hey, Mom," he greets, walking into the kitchen with Arizona in tow.

"Oh, there you are, dinner's almost ready," a pretty woman with ridiculously dark hair smiles over her shoulder at Jeremy from where she stands before the stove, before her eyes flit over to Arizona. Arizona smiles as nicely as she can and raises a hand in a tiny wave. Just as Jeremy's mother opens her mouth, another man strolls in. He looks to be the right age for being Jeremy's dad, but holds absolutely no resemblance to Arizona's boyfriend. His hair is the blondest blond there is—almost as blond as Arizona's, but not quite—and his eyes are he blackest black there is. When his eyes find Arizona, a slow, kind grin spreads onto his face.

"Oh," the man says, grin still intact. "So, you're Arizona?"

"Um, yessir," she smiles back uneasily, eyes questioning.

"Huh." He studies her face for a moment before nodding. "Well, I've only heard good things, so..."

Arizona turns to raise her brows pointedly at a now-flushed Jeremy. He rolls his eyes at her and she grins smugly. "Oh? He talks about me?" she says.

"All the time," this time another voice says, and Arizona sivels around to lock eyes with a pair of very blue ones. She gulps when she catches sight of the boy before her. He must be Jeremy's older brother; ignoring the fact that he has blue eyes instead of his younger brother's nice brown ones, they share slight similarities in their defined jaws and narrow-but-not-quite faces.

But while Jeremy is cute, this one is undeniably hot.

"Arizona," Jeremy sighs with a roll of his eyes, though he's smiling a tiny smile. "this is my brother. Jacob, Arizona."

"Hey," the older brother nods at her before snatching a carrot from the bowl on the counter, narrowly missing his mother's hand, which had been aimed towards his wrist. All Arizona can manage is a slight one of hers back. The faint shadow of a smirk kisses his lip as if he's aware of the unnatural effect his face has on her. He probably does, seeing as she is no doubt flushed all over, and that there is no way in hell this boy doesn't know how much like a Greek god he looks like. Arizona's body has this horrible habit of betraying her by blushing all over. And when she says all over, she means all over.

"Hi," she mutters, flicking her eyes away to the tan walls behind him. But it's as if he's a magnet of the opposite pole. Everything she looks at pulls her eyes back to him somehow. She has never felt so helpless before. Of all the boyfriends in the world, she just had to choose the one with a sexy brother. Holy fucking shit, she is so fucked.

Now, Arizona sits at the dining table, Jeremy next to her. Apparently, they always eat in the kitchen and/or on the living room couch in front of the TV, so this table is barely ever used—only for special guests. Arizona counts as a special guest, but while Mrs. Miller had informed her of that, Jacob had snorted quite loudly, to which Jeremy had responded with a glare. When Arizona had glanced at the older boy in confusion, he had only shaken his head, slight smirk lining his lips. It took quite a long time for her to pull her gaze away.

A second later, their mother comes bustling in, dish in hand. She sets it down in the center of the long table, grinning brightly and rubbing her hands together. "Okay, so, I made some wild rice, and it's my first time, so don't expect much."

"Oh, Good lord," Jacob mutters, leaning over for a plate nonetheless.

"Don't be rude," she says, flicking his head, and he ducks down, grinning. Arizona swears that for a second, her heart stops beating because of just how beautiful that fucking grin is. A second later, she calls for "Jane and Jessica!" and Arizona leans over to whisper to Jeremy.

"Do all your names start with a j?" she asks with amusement.

Jacob catches this from the other side of the table, where he sits, and answers before Jeremy can. He rolls his eyes, "Yeah. Who even said that was a good idea? I mean, parents already mix their kids' names up as it is, for fuck's sake."

"Don't curse at the dinner table," Mr. Miller grunts from the head of the table.

Just then, two girls come walking in, one in a black, lace skater dress, and one in a pair of jeans and a yellow t-shirt. Arizona knows the girl in the t-shirt, she does. She just can't place it. And then, it clicks and her eyebrows shoot up. The girl had been the one to serve her the last time at The Number.

"Oh, holy sh—" Here, Mr. Miller raises his eyebrows and she hurries to switch her words, "wow, you guys run The Number?"

"Yes, actually!" Mrs. Miller grins, pulling a chair out to sit in.

"That's cool. How come I never see you, Jeremy?" Arizona asks him before accepting the load of food Mrs. Miller is offering.

"I stay in the kitchen," he answers with a shrug. "And I'm not there much, either. Only on weekends, mostly."

"Oh. That's awesome, but what about that one brunette girl, I think her name's Beck? Or Becky? Her name doesn't start with a j, so I'm only guessing that she's not related to you." Jeremy and Jacob make a face at the same time, and she smirks.

"She's one of the only people my parents hire," he explains and Arizona nods.

"So, Arizona," his mom smiles a huge smile at her, which does little to help settle the nerves that have erupted again in her stomach. "You're in Jeremy's grade, right?"

"Um, yeah."

"And how about colleges? Which are you planning on applying to?"

"Oh, my god, Mom, stop scaring off all of Jeremy's girlfriends," the goth girl (who Jeremy informs her is Jane) mutters, stabbing at some chicken on her plate. Arizona's eyebrows rise and she smiles. Jeremy has had multiple girlfriends, then. Interesting. What's even more interesting, though, is that Arizona doesn't feel a thing. No pang of jealousy, no suspicion. And maybe, that's what scares her. Because, after all, girls are supposed to feel something for their boyfriends.

5

CHAPTER 5

It has been thirty-six days that Arizona and Jeremy have been dating. She knows this for sure because Crosley has been counting and the rest of her so-called friends have found that they enjoy counting with him. Despite this, they all say that she and Jeremy are a grenade ready to blow and they think that Arizona should get out when she can; they say that the aftermath might be quite cataclysmic. After meeting his parents, she had confessed to her friends that she doesn't feel anything for her boyfriend. Crosley had very helpfully informed her that she was screwed and the girls had hummed their agreement.

Of course, it really does not help that her parents demand to meet her boyfriend. Arizona has taken to peeking around corners to make sure that her mother is nowhere near the room she is about to enter and Lara, the oh, so very helpful Lara, has decided to watch the horror story unfold, finding it all too amusing.

Now, Arizona is splayed out on her bed, nose buried in a book. She is rereading the Harry Potter series and only God knows what round she is on. Probably somewhere in the thirteens. It is only normal that just as Harry is about to stab the diary with the tooth that her mother's voice calls for her. "What!" she hollers back. Her mother keeps yelling and keeps yelling back until Cora's voice gets so loud that she is screeching. Sighing, Arizona puts a pencil in the book to hold her place and heaves herself off the bed, out of the room, and up the stairs. This always happens. She's always the one who has to move so her mother can hear her—who called for Arizona first, mind you.

"What?" she asks now, standing before her mother where she sits reclined on the most comfortable couch in the living room.

"I'd really love it if you brought Jeremy home, you know," her mom smiles a kind smile and Lara, who is sitting in the corner, slowly lowers the magazine that had been obscuring her face prior to Arizona's arrival. A look that Arizona believes is far too evil settles over her sister's face as she watches the show unravel before her.

"God, Mom," Arizona groans, collapsing back onto the piano bench. She doesn't know why her parents decided to put the piano in the living room of all places. It takes up so much room. "We've only been dating for, like, a month. That's barely anything."

"Yes, but you met his parents already! It's only fair that we get to meet him."

"Yes, it's only fair, Zona," Lara repeats tauntingly from where she sits and Arizona turns to fix her with a glare.

"How old are you, two?" she snaps but Lara only smirks. "Shut up."

"Didn't say anything," Lara shrugs innocently and Arizona's scowl grows deeper.

"Yeah, but your face is just so goddamn irritating that I didn't rea—"

"Zona, hon', please?" Cora interrupts, knowing where her daughters' argument will go from here (that would be explicits and rude gestures).

Arizona stares at her mother's pleading face for a moment and her glare softens. Huffing, she throws her hands up in surrender. "Fine! Fine! I'll call him now, okay?"

"Oh, my god, thank you!" Cora squeals, much unlike the way forty-year-olds should act. "Lara, what should I make for him? This is so exciting! Our Zona got a boyfriend! Holy hell, this is the best." Waving with two fingers, Arizona irritably makes her way back to her room and aggressively pulls her phone out to call Jeremy.

And that is how Arizona May finds herself with her nose wedged in her closet again, everything resembling Valentine's Day just a tiny bit too much. "Ghah! What the hell do you wear—you know what, fine!" she growls to herself, pulling a pair of tights away from her face. "I'm just gonna wear a shirt and jeans because they're my parents and some—goddamn skirt, get away from me, you freak—random boy who I don't even like like that and holy shit what am I gonna do? What am I g—"

"Zona?"

"THAT'S NOT MY FUCKING NAME, LARA!" she screams without looking behind her. Her hair is a mess and the mascara she had decided to put on for the night is running everywhere it's not supposed to because of how much she's sweating (she sweats a lot when under pressure) and the last face she wants to see is the perfect one that belongs to her perfect fucking sister.

"Whoa," the older girl mutters, but makes no move to get out.

"What?" Arizona swirls on her heels, holding a clean pair of dark-wash jeans and a green, silk blouse. It's good enough, she makes up her mind. "Can you get out?" she asks bluntly. "I need to change."

"Okay. Then change."

"Can you get out?"

"You know," Lara muses, looking around, "normal sisters should be comfortable with changing around each other."

Arizona's mouth swings open. "What? Dude, just get out. We're not even normal sisters, for God's sake!"

"Okay, okay, jeez. I didn't remember you as this touchy."

"Lara, I am this close to touching you extra hard in the face with my fist if you don't get out right now," Arizona narrows her eyes and Lara's widen as she slowly backs out of the room, shutting the door. She doesn't leave, though, still talking from outside of Arizona's room.

"I was just supposed to tell you that Mom needs your help."

"Could you not have just said that?" Arizona yells incredulously, jumping up and down to tug the jeans up her legs. Zipping and buttoning it up, she pulls the blouse over her head and swings the door open abruptly. She wipes the mascara away from her eyes so that her face is completely bare now, because knowing her, more makeup will be useless since she'll probably start sweating like a cow in a slaughterhouse during dinner when her mother is so prone to asking stupid, personal questions.

"Whatever. Maybe this is why it took you so long to get a boyfriend. I still can't believe that you finally got a boyfriend, Zona!" Arizona winces at the nickname and what her lovely sister is hinting at. "It really is quite unbelievable, though," Lara raises her eyebrows and Arizona simply flips her off behind her back, climbing up the basement stairs to the main floor, where her mother cooks in the kitchen. She doesn't even care enough to retort, though she's burning up inside because her sister thinks she's just so much better than her.

"Why are you cooking so much, Mom?" she sighs exhasperatedly, peering over her mother's shoulder to see her preparing some kind of batter in a bit mixing bowl. "What are you even making?"

"We're having breakfast for dinner!" she exclaims brightly and Arizona blinks.

"Okay. Um. Well, Lara said you needed help?"

"Oh, yes!" Cora grins a blinding grin, brushing the stray hairs falling in front of her face back with her upper-arm, seeing as her hand is covered in pancake batter. "Could you put those hash-browns in the oven for 375 degrees, please? Thanks, babe."

Arizona does as she is told and just as she shuts the oven door, the doorbell chimes throughout the house. "Ooh!" he mom yelps excitedly. "Looks like Jeremy's here, huh? I'm gonna go get ready then. Go open the door, yeah?"

Sighing, Arizona walks towards the front door, ready to smile as kindly as she can. But the sight she is met with is quite the opposite of what she had been expecting. "Uh, where's Jeremy?" she asks slowly and Jacob shrugs, smiling a half smile, hands tucked into his pockets. Arizona forces herself to keep her eyes connected with his instead of roaming the rest of him.

"What, no hello?" he asks, smile fixed and Arizona sighs.

"Hello. So? Where is he?" she stands on her tiptoes to look behind him, but she sees no sigh of the boyfriend.

"He sent me here to say he couldn't make it. Apparently he lost your number, so he couldn't call to tell you himself."

"He lost my number," Arizona says dumbly.

"He lost your number," Jacob repeats in a affirmative tone, nodding slightly.

"Wow. How is that even possible?" Arizona had called him just the other day, how did he lose her number?

"Hey, that's what I said, too," Jacob grins and looks over his shoulder briefly before meeting Arizona's gaze again. "But, I just needed to tell you and now I should go, so—"

"Arizona? Is that him? Is that your perfect boyfriend?" Lara calls from the kitchen, interrupting the boy, and Arizona grinds her teeth together, jaw flexing. She's about to reply that he couldn't make that, but something takes over her mouth and the words yes, and it is pry their ways out of it. She watches as Jacob's eyebrows rise in a silent question. Giving him a look, she grabs onto his arm and pulls him into the house. He barely keeps himself from tripping over the threshold in surprise.

"Pretend to be my boyfriend just for tonight, and I swear I'll do whatever you want," she hisses, and soon a smirk replaces the look of surprise. Arizona actually has no idea what she is saying right now, but it seems like an okay idea. She just needs to prove to Lara that she is capable of getting a perfect boyfriend—and come on, everybody knows that Jacob is quite the example of that.

"Anything?" Jacob sighs, glancing down at his phone before slipping it back into his jeans' pocket.

"Within reason," she adds in a warning tone. "Now take your shoes off." He does as she says just as Lara makes her way through the kitchen doors and stands in the hall, leaning against the wall. Arizona bites back a grin when she catches her staring at the boy next to the younger girl for a bit longer than necessary.

"Lara!" Arizona grins too enthusiastically. "I want you to meet my boyfriend, Jac—Jeremy! Jeremy, this is my sister, Lara."

"Hey," he grins smoothly at Arizona's sister, who smiles back prettily. Arizona has the sudden urge to punch it off her face. She has a boyfriend, for fuck's sake.

"So, Jeremy," Ben starts, but Jacob doesn't look up. Of course he doesn't, his name isn't Jeremy. Arizona kicks his ankle sharply and his head snaps up with a startle. He smiles charmingly at her mother, who Arizona can swear swoons, and then her father, before kicking Arizona back, if a bit more gently. Arizona glares at him a small glare and he seems to catch it because she sees his grin widen. "Are you in college?"

When her mother had first seen Jacob (or, Jeremy), it had looked as if she might have pulled a muscle from how excited she had been. She had even nudged Lara, who had glared back. Though Ross might have felt suspicous, seeing as that Lara really was as sublte as a gunshot about how attractive she found Jacob, he found more humor in it than anything. Lara really doesn't know what she has.

"I'm actually taking a one-year break to help out at my family's restaurant, then going back next year," Jacob smiles, answering politely.

"Oh?" Lara raises a smug eyebrow and Arizona nearly throws up on her sister's cute ballet shoes, which she shouldn't be wearing, seeing as no one wears dirty shoes in the house. Then again, anything that is Lara's is dirty, except maybe Ross. "What are you planning to do when you go back?" Now that Lara has gotten over her attraction to Arizona's "boyfriend," she has been trying to find evey single fucking flaw in him—which, she is probably finding, proves pretty difficult because Jacob is kindasorta flawless. Which totally isn't okay, but whatever.

"Architecture, actually," he answers swiftly and Arizona relaxes back in her chair with a sigh. He's acomplished. Also, there's that thing where architects are hot. Shaking her head, she stuffs her mouth with pancakes, saving her from answering any questions from her own parents.

"Oh?" Lara seems to be thinking the same. "How old are you, again?"

"Legal," Jacob smirks and gaping, Arizona rams her foot into his ankle again, this time making him wince. Her parents stare at him blankly, blinking, and Lara flushes, clearly pleased. Ross clears his throat, still not feeling challenged. And maybe he's not. Glancing at Arizona, he nods the tiniest bit and engages her parents in conversation.

"Dude!" she hisses at Jacob, who simply looks at her, smirk still in place. "What the fuck, man? That was not okay! You're supposed to be my bo—"

"Well, uhm," Cora clears her throat, smiling again. "It really is quite exciting that you're Arizona's first boyfriend."

"Really? First boyfriend?" he says, eyebrows raised.

"Yeah," Arizona shifts in her seat, looking anywhere but him. "So?"

"Nothing," Jacob shrugs. "Just surprising, is all." Arizona's eyes snap up to his quickly and he grins, winking very unexpectedly. She feels her cheeks go off in an instance, and she can swear that her mother had just cooed. Hopefully, everyone has forgotten about his stupid comment towards Lara from before. When her parents retreat back into hushed conversations amongst themselves, Jacob leans back to murmer to Arizona. "Was that a good enough save?"

"I hate you," she states, but can't help the smile that is inching onto her lips.

"Funny," he says, looking at her with a smug expression. "You couldn't even look at me for two seconds last time without blushing like the sun."

"I don't even think that simile qualifies as a simile because no one can blush like the sun," she retorts, though she can feel her cheeks heating up all over again. He laughs quietly and she has to bite her lip hard to keep herself from thinking about how adorable the sound is. "Shut up," she snaps. "Quite flirting with me."

"Who's flirting with you? I'm not flirting with you."

"Every time you talk it sounds like you're flirting," she spits, though they both know that it's not much of an insult. Actually, it doesn't even make sense.

"Man, you're so in love with me."

"Can you not?"

"You're not denying it."

"Honestly, are you twelve?"

"No, I'm legal, remember?"

"I hate you," Arizona states in a matter-of-fact tone.

"Now, Arizona," he says in an overly patient tone. "I thought we'd gone over this; you're really in love with me."

"I'm going to the bathroom," Arizona announces and stands up suddenly, chair screeching back against the floor behind her and everyone looks at her. Smoothing her shirt down, she turns and walks out of the dining room, Jacob's quiet laughter following her.

6

— ◆ —

CHAPTER 6

"**N**ow tell me again, how did you think that was a good idea?" Romy leans against the locker next to Arizona's open one as the latter switches her textbooks for her backpack.

"Excuse you, I never said that it was a good idea," the blonde points out, slamming the locker door shut and swinging the bag over her shoulder. "I only summarized what I did."

"Dude, trust me on this," Romy flicks her fringe out of her eyes, "if you keep this up for any longer, everything's gonna blow up in your face." Arizona glances at her friend and feels an undeniable sinking feeling in her stomach.

"I know, I know. But there's something off about Jeremy, too, if you didn't notice."

"Dude, you think? How the fucking fuck does a guy lose his girl-friend's number? If he didn't want to see you he should have come up with a better excuse."

"Geez, thanks for the vote of confidence, Romy." Her friend only shoots her two thumbs up and an over-exaggerated grin.

"Don't mention it. Where are you going, now?" Romy slips out her phone to glance at something before sliding it back into her shorts' pocket.

"The Number. Meeting up with Alex."

"Oooh, fun, tell him Romy says hi," Romy grins and runs a hand through her hair, hoisting her shoulder back to a more comfortable position.

Arizona's mom's old husband is…interesting, for lack of better words. He thinks that Arizona might as well be his own daughter and when she was seven, he had dropped by for the first time.

Her mother doesn't mind that Arizona has quite a healthy relationship with her ex-husband, because the only reason they are divorced is that Alex is gay. Arizona can only imagine how hard it had been for her mother to be the one who made her husband realize that he is actually so very into the other gender, but the two are still relatively good friends. Alex's boyfriend is pretty awesome, too. "To see what my daughter would look like," Alex had said, though his real daughter would most probably look nothing like Arizona May, seeing as that basically nobody looks like Arizona May. But, it's not like she can complain, because Alex really isn't that bad. He's quite fun, actually. He's a writer. Alex always says to call him a writer, not an author (though, he has published quite a few novels), and when seven-year-old Arizona had asked why the hell he'd rather be called a writer than an author, he had handed her a dictionary and said, "look up the words."

So, she had, and it had taken forever because like any normal seven-year-old, she never really used dictionaries.

au·thor \ 'ȯ-ther \ n 1 : a person who writes or composes a literary work (as a book)

Seven-year-old Arizona couldn't find anything wrong with that, so she had flipped all the way to the w section to find the definition of writer. It has always been funny to her, how w was pronounced double u and it was a double u. She has, since then, grown out of these tiny things that amuse her, because Crosley had told her she was weird the first time she pointed out the little things she laughed at.

writ·er \'rit-er \ n 1 : AUTHOR 1 (here, she had laughed because the dictionary literally told the person to reference to the definition of author—which Alex had said was not the same as writer—which the dictionary then said it was.) 2 : one that can write

Seven-year-old Arizona had thought that there should have been some whole revolution that came upon her at that moment, as she shut the huge, blue dictionary with yellow pages, but there really wasn't. She had told Alex so, and he had made her sit down next to him on the brown carpet in his living room. She has always wondered why somebody in their right mind would ever choose a brown carpet over all the other colors.

"You see," Alex had started, "an author is someone who composes a book. But I am a writer, because a writer is one that can write. It's like the square-rectangle rule." The square-rectangle rule has always confused Arizona. "A square is a rectangle, but a rectangle is not a square," he had clarified. "Like that, an author is a writer, but a writer is not necessarily an author."

This theory has always been flawed to Arizona, though, because in the square-rectangle rule, the rectangle is never ever a square, but there is always a chance that the writer is an author. Seven-year-old Arizona had chosen the wise decision to not point this out to Alex.

"You don't have to publish a book to be a writer, Arizona," he had explained. Arizona has always liked him also because he is almost the only person left who calls her by her full name. "But you have to publish a book to be an author."

Still, the reasoning had been wrong, but the thought has stuck with Arizona because of the way Alex had told it to her. With so much sincerity and sureness and it was amazing for her to watch, because Arizona has never been so sure of anything before. She imagines that it's a wonderful feeling.

Now, she is approaching The Number, letters bold and luminous. Romy had left her some time along the way, turning right to her neighborhood. Only after entering and seeing the black-haired, light blue-eyed girl manning the register, does she remember that the restaurant is run by the Millers. Hoping that there will be no Jeremy and/or Jacob (emphasis on the Jacob) cameos today. She doesn't think she will be able to handle it. Jeremy's been as normal as can be at school but she still has no idea how to react to what happened with him losing her number and all. Not that it was a completely horrible thing, seeing as that she did get to spend some quality time with his quite attractive brother.

Swallowing thickly, she searches the small room before finding Alex in one of the booths over in the far corner, on the other side of the room. He sits with his back against the window, feet kicked up to cross at the ankles on the other end of the booth. He is reading a book with his natural book-reading face: eyes kind of squinted, eyebrows creased, lips pursed, chin tucked into his neck. Arizona can see what his boyfriend, Chris, finds so endearing. Painting on a grin, she walks over, combat boots tapping against the hard floor. Jessica, from behind the counter, looks up at this and locks eyes with Arizona, so she has no choice but to wave and smile at the dark girl. To her surprise, Jessica smiles back, nodding barely. She's not so unapproachable, after all.

Reaching the booth, she taps Alex's shoe with a finger and he jerks up from where his eyes had been transfixed on the words. "Arizona!" he cries, instantly scrambling up to tug her in for a hug. The book he had been reading before (Arizona reads the title as The Joke by Milan Kundera), lays now-forgotten on the table. Though he's a tall and lean man, his character has always reminded her of a much more toned-down version of Joey Tribbiani*. He's a dark blond with blue eyes, jaw usually scruffy, hand constantly pushing his hair back out of his eyes. His smile is infectious and he was obviously quite the heartbreaker when he was younger; funny how he turned out not liking girls. Cora has always told Arizona that the gorgeous gays are the worst, because some of them aren't even aware of their sexuality and end up breaking your heart because of it. Arizona couldn't have helped but laughed the first time her mother had told her the story of her ex-husband.

"Hey, Alex," she grins, pulling back, and he slides back into his side, waving for her to take a seat opposite to him.

"How've you been?" he asks. "I ordered a hot chocolate for you in case Cora's still all about not having caffeine before you're in college."

"Oh, yeah, she's still insane," Arizona grins and he chuckles. "And it's okay, I guess. I got a boyfriend, which is weird."

"Oooh, tell me more," Alex sits up and leans towards her. Though he doesn't resemble much of the gay stereotypes in books and such what with the sixth sense in fashion, impeccable hair, and pretty scarves, he can jump easily into the character when he wants to. That's one of the greatest things about him, Arizona thinks.

"Thing is," she sighs, smiling uncertainly, "he has kind of a really attractive older brother and I have no idea what I'm doing because I'm not really very into Jeremy in that way."

"Wait, who's Jeremy, again?"

"Oh, he's the boyfriend. And Ja—"

"Here's the drinks," another very familiar voice interrupts and stifling a gasp, Arizona jumps in her seat, leaning back, away from Alex. Her heart is pounding and her chest is heaving. Shit. It's Jacob and he looks only ten times hotter with a black apron tied around his neck and his hair extra chaotic. "Oh, hey, Arizona," he smirks at her, who can do nothing but blush and stutter a greeting back. She could have sworn that she had gotten over whatever this was since the dinner, but apparently not. "I'm Jacob." He introduces himself to the man across from Arizona.

"Oh, hello," Alex says back, almost flirtatiously, and Arizona kicks him slightly under the table. His eyebrows rise in a seemingly innocent questioning look. "I'm her mother's ex-husband. But Arizona and I are best friends, right, Arizona? Right. Are you a friend of Arizona's?"

"Future brother-in-law, actually."

Alex's mouth creates a circle and eventually spreads out into a cheeky grin. He looks about ready to burst out laughing and Arizona slams her head down on her arms crossed over the table, hair billowing out around her. Why is it that everybody around her loves inflicting pain on her? "Well, actually," Alex says with a cocked brow, "I think there's more of a chance of your brother being t—"

"Alex!" Arizona glares at the man who chuckles and shakes his head.

"Sorry, sorry. Thanks for the drinks, Jacob." After a glance and smirk thrown to Arizona (because there is no point in trying to talk to a girl who has poured half a mug of piping hot chocolate into her mouth to avoid conversation) and a nod to Alex, Jacob turns and heads back to the kitchen, disappearing behind the swinging doors. "He's cute," Alex says in a stage whisper. Arizona swallows, burning her tongue in the process, and releases a long breath and Alex wiggles his eyebrows at her and she does her best to look angry, but no one can't really stay mad at Alex. As quickly as the smug expression comes, it leaves, and suddenly he is incredibly excited, leaning forwards, closer to Arizona.

She blinks. "What?"

"I got this new typewriter and holy shit, Arizona, I feel so hipster but I think it's the best thing that has ever happened to me after discovering myself. Oh! And also, I brought you a present."

"What? Alex, no, why do you do that?"

He waves her protests away. Alex always brings Arizona something every time they meet, and they're usually the best things, but Arizona is always left feeling guilty because she never remembers to get him something, too. Now, Alex unfolds his jacket lying on the seat next to him, and draws a book out. He places it gently before Arizona and rests his chin on his palms, urging her on to look at it. She does.

"The MiraculousJourney of Edward Tulane by Kate DiCamillo," he says, motioning towards the small book. "It's my brother's favorite book. He made me read it and I actually really loved it. And I think that you might, too."

"Wow, thanks, Alex." She grins at him.

"It's fine. Just don't show your mom, yeah?" he winks in a conspiratorial manner and Arizona laughs, nodding. Most of the presents Alex gives her end up being books because he loves reading as much as Arizona does. Cora has steadily been getting more and more impatient with the amount of books in her daughter's room, and Alex's addings haven't really been helping. "Now about this hot older brother."

"No."

7

Chapter 7

When Jeremy Miller invites Arizona May over for dinner with his family she asks why. He explains that his brother is in town—has been for a few weeks—and his parents are insisting on having a small dinner party, and it is only natural for him to invite his girlfriend.

"There'll be other families there, too," he says, "so you can bring yours, too."

"No!" she exclaims a bit too quickly, a bit too loudly.

Jeremy blinks. "Oh, uh, okay. Anyway, it'll be at The Number 'cause my mom doesn't want to clean the house. So."

"Yeah!" she paints on a blinding grin. "Yeah, of course."

Though, in the inside she is shaking her head intensely. See, Lara along with the rest of her family, are under the (incorrect) impression that Jacob is her boyfriend, when it's actually Jeremy who is. God only knows what will go down when they find out the truth—not that they will, especially Lara. Arizona will make sure of it.

And that is how Arizona finds herself standing in the entrance of the restaurant under the descending suns, clad in the nicest non-dress she could find. The pound cake her mother had baked sits heavily (no pun intended) in her upturned palms and the toes of her shoes pull down the rising cuffs of her jeans down back over her ankles. She is not sure whether to knock on the door or go in or what. The sign hanging behind the glass says Closed, so that no one but the guests come in, and shrugging, she pushes the door open. It's unlocked.

"Arizona!" It's Mrs. Miller. She's smiling a terribly wide smile, eyes glimmering with excitement, hair frizzing up around her face. There are already some people milling around and Arizona is relieved to find that she didn't overdress, nor did she underdress. Arizona smiles back, giving an awkward wave which soon gets crushed when Mrs. Miller crushes her to her chest in a warm embrace. "How are you? Oh, my god, is this for me? That's lovely, thank you, thank you. It looks delicious. Did your mom make it? Oh, there's Jeremy—Jeremy! Arizona's here, hun'." And then she is being pushed towards the amused-looking boy walking towards her.

"Hey," he grins at Arizona, also hugging her before pulling back and scanning her head to toe. "You look very pretty."

"Why do you sound so patronizing?" Arizona narrows her eyes at him and he smirks, throwing his hands up in the air.

"Who sounds patronizing? I'm not patronizing."

"Whatever," she laughs. "Thanks, I guess."

"You're welcome. Are you not going to compliment me?"

"No," Arizona mumbles jokingly as her eyes survey the room. It's been transformed, tables pushed up into one giant dining table in the center of the restaurant, and it looks almost elegant with the blinds drawn shut and festive lights hung up around.

"Why don't you two go help Jeremy's brother in the kitchen," Mrs. Miller suggests, showing up again, and Arizona nearly chokes on her spit.

"Jacob's cooking?"

"Oh, sure! He always does the cooking here—god knows that it's much better than mine," she winks and Arizona's face flushes, though there is literally no reason this time. What the fuck. Maybe it's the idea of Jacob in a chef's hat and apron, whisking around the kitchen, and how funny and—well, hot it is.

Jeremy and Arizona are helping Jacob in the kitchen, and much to Arizona's surprise and amusement, Jacob is very serious when cooking. He doesn't speak, only muttering occasionally for them to bring him this and taste that. Arizona's mind had been right; he is quite attractive when doing so.

"Here, go set up the table," he directs Jeremy, now, sparing him barely a glance. Shrugging, Jeremy does as he's told, slipping off the stool, grabbing a stack of ceramic plates and china, then hurrying out of the kitchen. Pursing her lips, Arizona clears her throat awkwardly and sits, watching Jacob for a few minutes as he finishes up whatever he's doing in one of the pots.

"So, you cook," she states after moments of silence and literally slaps her leg under the table where Jacob can't see, because of just how fucking dumb she sounds. Jacob pauses to look at her with raised eyebrows and tilted lips.

"I do."

"Hot."

"What?"

Another slap to her leg.

"It's hot. Aren't you hot there, near the stove?" she fumbles, somehow getting a cohesive sentence out without stumbling. Sad thing is, whenever the triumph happens to Arizona, her face is always there to betray her with the terrible blush it develops.

"Oh, yeah," he blinks, but she is one hundred and one percent sure that he is smirking at her. "But I'm hot all the time, so moving away from the stove won't really change anything," he tells her in a matter-of-fact tone, turned away as he stirs the pot's contents. Arizona rolls her eyes and throws a nearby fork at him, but it harmlessly bounces off of his (quite deliciously broad) shoulders. So, she huffs audibly, instead. When he turns around, again, Jacob is grinning an infuriating grin. "So, what's up with your name?" he asks, finally, and Arizona's eyes flit up from where they focus on her tangled fingers.

"Beats me," she snorts. "I can't quite fathom how drunk my parents must have been the night they decided to name me after a state and a month."

"That is pretty harsh," he agrees with dark, furrowed brows. He draws the spoon out of the soup he has been stirring to lick it and place it in the sink. Arizona fights hard to keep her eyes away from his very pink, very kissable lips.

Now, she watches as Jacob rubs at a stain on one of the many glasses set out on the counter, arms flexing under his black shirt's sleeves, forearms tensing. Holy shit, how do forearms even look so attractive? Dear God, where the hell is Jeremy?

"You," he pauses mid-wipe to point a finger at her, and his eyebrows rise, again. "you need a nickname."

"uh," she shifts foot to foot, looking everywhere but him because God knows what kind of thoughts she would think if she stares at him for more than a second.

"Ari?" he muses, breathing on the glass and wipes at it, clearing away the gray fog. "Zona? Riz? Ri? Ar? Zo? Na?"

"You're just breaking my name up," she rolls her eyes and his eyes flick back up to meet hers, quick smile flitting onto his lips and leaving just as fast.

"That's the point of a nickname, Zona."

"Eugh, we're going with Zona?" Arizona wrinkles her nose and he pouts. She bites down on her lip hard.

"What? I quite like it." He turns away so she has a great view of his black t-shirt-clad back, and switches the now-shiny glass for another. Then, Jacob leans back to rest on the counter, legs crossed at the ankles. Arizona's breath comes out as a relieved whoosh when Jeremy enters, saving her from having to constrain her mouth so it doesn'ts blurt out anything stupid. That seems to be happening a lot lately.

"Quite like what?" Jeremy asks mindlessly, ambling towards the sink to place some dirty dishes into it with a clatter.

"My new cupcake recipe," Jacob answered smoothly. So smoothly, in fact, that Arizona can't help but wonder how many times he has lied like that. She does her best to ignore the adorable fun fact that Jacob bakes to go along with his cooking. He shoots her a quick wink before flicking the back of his brother's head lightly in a flamboyant manner and strolling lazily out of the swinging double doors, tray of water glasses balanced on his right hand.

Jennifer Miller, the oldest of the siblings, is here and just like the rest of the family, she is absolutely gorgeous. Arizona's self esteem is slowly sinking lower and lower the more she spends time with the Millers; it really isn't fair at all. But, much to her pleasure and relief, Jennifer is the absolute opposite of Lara. She's nice and sweet and doesn't totally look down upon Arizona for being—God forbid—younger than her.

"So," she says now, smiling a kind smile, her dark brown eyes lighting up. "Do you do anything? Like, hobbies or sports?"

"Well, I, um, I'm looking for a job right now, actually. I mean, I volunteer at the Rehab center, and that's great, but I kind of need money, you know?" Jennifer laughs lightly and nods.

"Arizona plays piano," Jacob says suddenly, appearing next to the two girls. Arizona's eyebrows rise as she studies him skeptically.

"Said who?"

"There was a piano at your house."

"Doesn't mean I play."

"Do you, though?"

"I...can," Arizona flicks her eyes somewhere else. She hasn't touched the piano in years. Her parents had signed her up for lessons in the first grade but she had never really enjoyed it much. Quitting was one of the happiest days of her life. "But I don't." She braces herself for the next questions but instead, Jacob only studies her warily, eyes going from corner to corner of her face.

"When did you go to her house?" And then Jeremy is there, too, waiting patiently for the answer along with his older sister.

"When you ditched on her and lost her phone number?" Jacob makes big eyes at Jeremy, who flushes immediately, a look of guilt suddenly hung over his face.

"Right. I'm really sorry about that, Arizona," he gives her a half smile. Jacob scoffs almost incredulously but Arizona ignores it, waving away the other boy's apology. "It's just that I had to help my parents at The Number because Friday's always really crowded and—"

"Dude, it's fine," Arizona laughs, interrupting him.

Only after the words are out does she truly realize how hard she just friendzoned her boyfriend. From what she knows, none of her friends call their boyfriends dude. Gem doesn't call Crosley dude. Jacob and Jennifer seem to understand at the same time, eyebrows rising, mouth making and o shape. Jacob looks about ready to burst out laughing, but Jeremy is still as oblivious as ever, happy just to not have pissed Arizona off.

After that, the two boys amble off so that it's just Arizona and Jennifer, again. "So, you were saying?"

"Oh!" Arizona blinks. "Oh, yeah, um, so I'm just looking for a paying job right now, because I'm just a little bit broke."

"You know, my parents are hiring right now, looking for any other people who'll be willing to work. I can tell them that you want to, I'm sure they'd be perfectly happy to give you a spot."

"Oh, my God, really? That would be amazing," Arizona grins and Jennifer nods. Mr. Miller seems to overhear because at least one person this household will always overhear any conversation, it's so large, and he smiles widely.

"The job's yours," he says and Arizona doesn't know whether she is jealous or sympathetic of Jeremy for living in this house, because it is just so incredibly dysfunctional.

Jeremy insists on walking Arizona out after the dinner. He tells her that Jacob is planning on throwing a party in two weeks, when their parents will be gone to some distant relative's wedding or something. "My mom said to invite you." His parents knowing about this party and being totally fine with it is really very weird.

"Oh, so inviting me is a chore, is it?" Arizona teases, smiling, and he rolls his eyes. She steps out of the door, standing on the sidewalk and the two stare at each other for a moment. Jeremy crosses his arms and leans against the wall next to him.

"It kind of is," he raises his eyebrows at her and with a laugh, he winds his arms around her for a hug. Arizona wishes it weren't like this, thought, because her feelings towards Jeremy are on the same level as her feelings towards Crosley—completely platonic.

But, maybe they'll grow! They're bound to, if she continues spending this much time with him.

Right?

8

CHAPTER 8

Crosley is ignoring Arizona. He had been absent at lunch and she just really needed to talk to him, so she had gone off on a search for him. She found him sat at a long, gray, plastic table in the library, head hidden behind an unnaturally large textbook. And now he is ignoring her.

"Crosley," she stage-whispers in a volume well near that of a whine.

He doesn't say anything, only flipping the page over.

"Dude. Hey. Crosley. What the hell, man."

"I'm studying, Arizona."

Crosley is very, very serious about his studies. He has this huge, cliché dream of running off to New York after graduating, but in place of pursuing a career in acting or music or the likes, he wants to attend Columbia for law. Arizona is not sure why he can't do that one state down in California or something. The suburbs of Oregon aren't totally shitty. And it's not totally tiny that everyone knows everything or anything; it's nice, with everything in walking distance and downtown only twenty minutes away.

"I'm having a crisis, Cros."

"Huh. So is everyone else, you self-centered asshole."

"Rude." But Arizona knows that Crosley is never serious about insults towards anyone except the people he despises. Or the really dim girls who don't know sarcasm when it punches them in the boob.

"Fine," he sighs much too dramatically, shutting the book with a heavy thud and swiveling his butt on the chair to face Arizona. "How may I help you, Arizona May." His smile is strained and she rolls her eyes. When his eyebrows rise she lunges forward in panic and shakes her hands in the air.

"I didn't mean it! I didn't mean the eye roll! I swear."

"Right. What's this crisis, then?"

"Jeremy has a really hot older brother."

"Really."

"Really."

Crosley looks at her for a second before laughing a tiny, short laugh and shaking his head, glancing down at his finger tapping a pencil against the table. "Didja sleep with him?"

Arizona chokes on her spit and Crosley watches in silent amusement, being absolutely no help at all. "No?" she gasps finally and he smirks, leaning back in the chair. "I just—Crosley, I don't like Jeremy and I'm scared to break up with him because he's just so sweet—"

"We are talking about the same Jeremy-Who-Lost-His-Girlfriend's-Phone-Number, right?"

"Uh...yeah?"

"Okay. So then why can't you dump him?"

"Because! He's really nice."

"Ten bucks says he's not and he's actually cheating on you and/or ditched you that night he "lost your number"." Crosley makes finger quotation marks and big eyes at her.

Arizona frowns. "What? Crosley, that's not—not the issue. And it's not true."

"See!" he exclaims softly. "There it is. If you actually liked Jeremy, you would be much more concerned about this. But you're not. So just ditch the asshole like he did to you and fuck his brother and be done with it."

"You're such a guy," Arizona wrinkles her nose up.

"It's called reasonable. And if you don't want to talk to a guy, then don't talk to a guy."

"How does Gem like you? Seriously."

"I'd be offended except she doesn't like me."

Then, Arizona makes a sudden, spur-of-the-moment decision and turns excitedly towards the boy once again. "I'll make you a deal. If you suck up your bullshit and ask Gem out—not before telling us that we were right—I'll break up with Jeremy."

"Or, we could do it the opposite way. You break up first."

"SO YOU DO LIKE HER!" Nearby students turn to glare at her and she ducks down sheepishly with a tiny sorry. "Fine," she grins, saying in a much mellower tone. "Deal."

Jeremy is gone from school that day, almost like a sign. But as Arizona is his chemistry partner, she must take the homework to him. Well, it's not really anyone's fault but hers; she offered. She brings it to The Number with her on Saturday, the next day. She's been working the morning shift for a couple of weeks so far.

Walking to the corner, she slides her apron over her head and ties it behind her before heading towards the kitchen, usually where one can find Jeremy. But, much to her annoyance, the door doesn't budge. She bangs her fist against it a couple times and hears footsteps heading towards her from the inside. Jacob opens it suddenly and Arizona nearly falls in, just barely steadying herself. Jacob looks very tired and very, very shirtless.

"Didn't realize it was locked," he mutters, meeting her gaze dead-on. Jacob always does that, looks straight into the other person's eyes, and Arizona doesn't know whether it's endearing or a bit uncomfortable. As of now, it is extremely uncomfortable.

"What are you doing?" her question comes out strangled and overly-dramatic, though neither of them have any idea why.

"Uh," Jacob's eyes flicker down to his bare chest, where she is looking, then back to her, blinking. "There are many correct answers to that. Living, breathing, stand—"

"Haha," she shoots him a look, pushing past him into the room, trying her best to not pass out when her very bare arm comes into contact with his very bare body. "Where's Jeremy? I brought him his chemistry homework," she holds up the folder and his eyebrows rise.

"He's gone," Jacob says, sauntering back into the kitchen.

"Hey, could you, maybe put a shirt on, pretty please?" she asks, eyes narrowed as they follow his very very nice back muscles. Fuck.

"No."

"You're an ass." Though, it is quite warm deeper into the kitchen.

"M'kay."

"Ass," she mutters, following him into the kitchen and taking the stool that she had sat in last time. "Where is he?" she asks curiously, watching him pile God knows what onto a slide of bread and placing a nother piece at the top. Jacob glances over his horrendously beautiful shoulder at her.

"Probably fucking some college girl," he shrugs nonchalantly and for the second time that day, Arizona chokes.

"Sorry, what?" He shrugs again. "It's amazing, how much faith you put in our relationship," she comments with a look and he turns to peer at her. The stare-off lasts for a few super long seconds before he blinks.

"Okay, that previous answer obviously wasn't true," he rolls his eyes, dragging out a stool across from Arizona on the other side of the island and sitting his nice butt on it. Jacob raises doubtful eyebrows at her (how does someone convey a feeling with their eyebrows, anyway?) and smirks. Suddenly quite awkward, she picks at the cracks between the marble tiles on the counter. "But, you do know my brother's a manslut, right?" he speaks up and Arizona is surprised she doesn't snap her head off at how fast she raises it to look at him.

"Who, Jeremy?" she scoffs incredulously and he shakes his head as if he pities Arizona and laughs just the tiniest bit.

"Arizona May," he almost sighs.

"I thought you were calling me Zona?"

"I decided that I like Arizona May much better. Pretty laughable," he replies without the blink of an eye, before transitioning quite smoothly into his next question, "Have you not seen how many girls he's had in the last year alone?"

"Um, no?"

"I'll tell you," he grunts, leaning over the counter from the other side so their faces are, like, five inches apart. His eyes seem lighter. His lips more kissable. Him more fucka—whoa. What? "El-e-ven." Jacob's mouth pronounces it carefully, in chunks, as if any quicker and Arizona might not understand. She snaps back, eyebrows furrowed.

"That's impossible. Jeremy? My Jeremy?"

"Yes, your Jeremy," he rolls his eyes with just the smallest hint of annoyance held in his voice.

"Wow. I guess I underestimated him."

"That's all you have to say about it?" He looks at her in the weirdest way and she shrugs this time.

"What do you want me to say? That they're all whores and I hate them? You want me to call your own brother a slut in front of you? I'd rather not get beat up by you, thanks."

"Please," he snorts as if that's the most out-of-the-world thought he had ever heard. "like I would ever touch a girl."

"Okay," Arizona raises a brow, ignoring his last comment, "then how many girlfriends have you had?"

"One," he told me simply and she blanches. He's screwing with her.

"One this year?"

"Once this life."

"What?" he shrugs, looking slightly amused. "What happened to her?"

"Well, I...uh...we were kind of...fiances at some point?" he says it as more of a question and Arizona tries not to think about how adorable he looks right now, scratching the back of his neck. It's not that hard to distract herself, though, after listening to what he just said.

"You were engaged? What happened to her?" She asks for the second time and he looks everywhere but her for the first time in however long she's known him.

"She cheated on me."

"Oh, that sucks," Arizona bites her lip, unsure whether to hug him or not. It would be so awkward. 'Specially since he's fucking shirtless, and all. "Who'd she cheat on you with?" Silence. Then,

"Jeremy."

Arizona is way beyond surprise by now, but she stays quiet for a moment, studying his face closely.

"Jeremy, as in your-brother-my-boyfriend Jeremy?"

"That's the one." It's so hard to believe and she is so so fucking confused as to when this happened. It's not like she's particularly angry at Jeremy because she doesn't think she has many romantic feelings towards him yet, anyway.

But... "But how are you guys not in the midst of some dramatic brother rivalry, then?" She asks honestly and he smirks.

"Because them cheating on me made me realize how dumb she was. In every sense possible. I mean, yeah it was an incredibly huge dick move on his part, but he's a guy and he's my brother, and both of those people make mistakes. And I never really loved Jan—my ex—much, anyway. I think it was just the fact that I knew her so well, why not stay with her, you know? Jeremy's a douchebag, yeah, but she was a slut, anyway. And I've done my fair share of asshole moves, too. Not that I don't want to get back at him or anything," he adds as an afterthought.

"Oh? So you want to steal one his girlfriends?"

His eyes snap back to Arizona's and suddenly, she finds it terribly, unfairly difficult to breathe. "That wouldn't be so bad. Depends on the girlfriend." Just as he's about to turn back to where he had been standing before, Arizona speaks up again.

"Are you trying to say that you're not a slut then?"

"I never said that either."

"You just said that you've only had one girlfriend in your entire life."

"Yeah. Girlfriend." When he winks, she scrunches her nose up in disgust.

"Oh, gross."

"Please, you love it."

"Pig," she snorts instead, grabbing the waiting tray of hot chocolates in her right hand, and exiting the swinging kitchen doors, because, never in a million years will Arizona admit that she does actually kind of really love it.

9

CHAPTER 9

Working at the rehabilitation center is actually more fun than one might think. Arizona isn't quite sure what she works as, actually, but it's fun nonetheless. Maybe the fact that a lot of the patients, if not most of them, are more like characters than they are people. After working here for a nearly a year so far, she is still trying to understand them.

Right now, she is in the center of watching James paint. With his glasses, short blonde hair, painting, and reading, he is probably by far the nicest person she has ever met and gotten to know. But, then again, it's not like he has much competition seeing as all Arizona's friends are dipshits. He refuses to tell her what he is painting all the time, so every time she comes, she always spends just a little bit of time trying to figure out what it is being brushed onto the canvas. Arizona has about as much of an idea as she did a week ago: none. Adeeb, James' best friend, sits across from Arizona at her table, knitting what he claims will be a pair of mittens. He, on the other hand, is the complete opposite of James with his dry sense of humor and perpetually rolling eyes and sarcastic commentary.

"Wait, so is that, like, a d—"

"Arizona May!"

Said girl's head whips around immediately and does not really know what she's thinking when her eyes settle on who is Jacob fucking Miller. He, of course, looks as good as ever. Just then, Arizona sneezes a loud sneeze, barely covering it with her elbow in time. But it is loud enough to draw the attention from Adeeb and James. Also, a "bless you" from the latter. Following her line of gaze, the two boys see the one in the entrance at the same time, and as James lowly says,

"Oooooooooooooooh."

Adeeb yelps,

"WHO IS THAT, ARIZONA MAY?"

"No one," Arizona uncomfortably shifts and clears her throat, not knowing if she should get up or not, though Jacob has made it incredibly clear that she should.

"Mhm," Adeeb raises his eyebrows and James grins.

"He's hot," says another voice which belongs to Lisa, another resident girl here. But, last time Arizona checked, Lisa was a lesbian.

"You're gay, Lisa," sighs Adeeb, and Arizona nods in confirmation to herself, still avoiding eye contact with Jacob. He's dressed in a gray thermal shirt clinging to his chest in the hottest way possible and the sleeves pushed up to his elbows and his hands jammed into the pockets of dark wash jeans and a beanie and fuck beanies have always been Arizona's undoing and fuck he looks good.

"So?" Lisa flicks the back of Adeeb's head, making him wince away with a tiny ow. "I can still think guys are hot. Don't you think some guys are super attractive even though you're straight?" she asks and Adeeb develops a what the fuck look.

"No?"

"Yeah, you do, Deebs," James rolls his eyes.

"What the hell did you just call me?"

"Dee—"

"That's not a fucking name!" Adeeb then proceeds to attack James, grabbing him in a headlock and James' butt sticks in the air. "Mmph, id—"

"What the hell!"

"You guys need to calm down," Arizona raises her eyebrows and slowly, Adeeb slides of James, who's grinning like mad.

"Go paint your ass," Adeeb mutters to the other boy. "Bet you have a great view from where your HEAD'S STUCK!" his voice grows louder steadily and James just laughs.

"Touchy."

"Touchy," he makes a face, mocking James in an exaggerated falsetto voice.

In the car, she turns the radio on and he turns to look at her with a horrified expression. After the whole Adeeb/James debacle, Jacob had spoken up from the door to inform Arizona that he was there to pick her up for Jeremy—who was supposed to pick her up on the way to work. Jacob had said that Jeremy was at a doctor's appointment. Now, Jacob looks at her with this look in his eyes, as if she is the craziest person ever for turning the music on.

This is 101.3 kink, thanks for listening and I hope you guys ha—

"What?" Arizona blinks.

"You do not turn on the radio when there is a perfectly good CD in the player," he says in a duh tone. Arizona raises her eyebrows and throws her hands up in the air in a surrendering position.

"I'm sorry."

"Good," he sniffs, pressing the CD button.

Weirdo.

Arizona doesn't know what song is playing now (until Jacob says that it's called Uma, not even bothering to mention the artist.) The silent air between them is thick and though it's not suffocating, it's so sufficiently awkward that it is getting there. Jacob, apparently feeling the same way, finally clears his throat.

"So. How's my brother?"

"Why are you asking me, he's your brother."

"Yes, and he's your boyfriend."

"Eh."

"What?" he turns and blinks at Arizona, who refuses to meet his gaze and instead looks out the window. The spring rain taps on the glass like a thousand fingers.

"I just..." she stops again and watches from the corner of her eye as he rolls his own, letting out a frustrated sigh.

"Girls. All the same, never finishing those goddamn sentences. Just tell me."

"Promise you won't tell Jeremy?"

"If you actually thought I'd tell him, you wouldn't even be making me promise right now," the sass queen points out and Arizona stares at him hard until he throws his right hand off the steering wheel flippantly. "Fine, whatever, I promise."

"Okay. I just...I just don't really like him like that."

He gasps dramatically like a schoolgirl. "What, you mean like like?"

Thwacking him on the arm, she nods grudgingly. "Yes, like like. I just don't. I've been trying to, too, believe me."

"Why are you telling me this?"

Her eyes grow. "What do you mean why am I telling you this, you asked!"

"No, I asked how he is. Not how you think of him. It's going to be so hard not to mock him about it, now. His girlfriend doesn't like him. Damn, that's harsh."

"You promised you wouldn't tell him!" she cries, voice steadily rising to an octave a bit too high for both their ears'. She ignores his cringe.

"I'm kidding, God, calm down." He laughs a breathy laugh and she smacks him lightly again. This time, he hits her back and though it's as gently as she did to him, if not lighter, she lets out a loud yelp. Jacob's head swivels in her direction immediately, face painted in panic. "Shit, I didn't mean to hurt you, are you okay?"

"You hurt me," Arizona wails and his eyes grow even larger, face completely distressed. He switches from looking at the road and her face. When she can't handle it anymore she bursts out laughing and frowning, he eases back into his seat.

"God. Such an asshole," he mutters.

"Excuse me?"

"You're excused."

"Grow up."

"I'm older than you. You grow up."

"Wow amazing comeback, damn, how do you come up with this genius?" she claps her hands slowly and he smirks.

"That's what everyone says," he shrugs and Arizona rolls her eyes, unable to keep the smile off her lips. "One more thing: if you want to convince everyone else that you're in love with my brother, you might wanna try harder."

"What—you knew?"

"I could guess."

Arizona curses and the stupid boy laughs.

The bells jingle against the door as it opens once again. Jessica is at the couple that just entered's table promptly. The café is packed again today and Arizona wants nothing more than to go home and read in her warm bed. Alas, she has a strong need for money and also this huge terrible thing called homework presently scattered before her on the counter she is leaned over. Suddenly a kick is aimed at the back of her knees with an irritatingly amused warning of "Oh, don't fall!"—anyone's weak spot—and just as she starts collapsing an arm steadies, unlike her heart which is beating it's way out of her chest.

"What the fuck," she hisses whipping around, only to stop when she meets the much too blue gaze of Jacob. She can't breathe, and he's smirking. "Don't—don't do that. Don't you know you're not supposed to do that to someone? God."

He laughs, patting her shoulder in a teasing manner before walking around to stand on the other side of her, peering over her shoulder at the paper in front of Arizona. He smells of coffee and paper and rain and boy and it is all she can sense and she just wants to melt back into his chest and stay there forever but she can't because this is her fucking boyfriend's fucking older brother goddammit. What did Arizona ever do to ask for this in her life?

"Whatcha doing?" he asks in a voice way too innocent for him. Arizona clears her throat.

"I, uhm. Homework."

"What class?"

"AP Enviro."

"Hey, I took that class freshman year, is Neal still teaching?"

"Yeah, I have her."

"Nice, I liked her."

"Yeah, she's cool."

The topic is so mundane that Arizona is really freaking confused as to if this is actually Jacob or not.

"Do you need help, or something?" He asks then, and Arizona nearly falls from surprise.

Jacob is suddenly being very inexplicably nice to her and Arizona squints at him. "I'm just, uh, annotating this article and then I have to answer some questions or whatever. Just a lot of reading, I guess."

"O-o-okaaay."

Arizona glares at him. "What?"

"Nothing. You just looked confused, that's all."

"Well, I'm not."

"Okay," he shrugs.

"Fine."

"Fine." He smirks.

"Whatever."

The door opens again and Arizona glances up, only to grin widely when she sees Crosley and Gem step over the threshold, Crosley shaking droplets off of (the one) umbrella and wrapping it up again. Arizona bites back the smirk as she approaches their booth after sharing a glance with Jacob.

"Hey, loooovebirds," she cooes and Gem's head snaps up.

"You sound like a forty-year-old mother you see on TV," she glares at Arizona, who only laughs.

"Whaddya guys want then," she winks at Crosley, whose face immediately bursts into every shade of red. He's so in deep with Gem, it's kinda really freaking adorable. Gem says she wants a peppermint hot chocolate with extra whipped cream, and when Arizona points out that this is, in fact, extra expense, Gem shrugs and grins and says "That's okay, Crosley's paying for me." Arizona barely just stifles the huge grin threatening to break over her lips. Her lips might just be bleeding from how hard she is biting them. When asked in an exaggerated voice what Crosley would like, he sends Arizona the scariest yet funniest death glare before muttering that he'll just have the same. Arizona can't help it anymore and lets herself laugh just the tiniest bit. Crosley trips her on her way back to the counter, where Jacob is hunched over, looking at the reading Arizona had been doing for class.

Sensing her near him, he looks up, and he slowly smiles a crooked smile, and Arizona tries her best to ignore the adorable way his eyes crinkle around the corner. He wiggles his brows at her. "Wow, they're almost as cute as us."

"I'm sorry, what?" Arizona nearly chokes.

"I'm just kidding, calm down. I helped you with your homework, by the way."

Handing the order sheet to him, Arizona gently pushes him to the side to glance over her article and finds the most useless questions taking up nearly the entirety of the margins, literally just questioning every freaking thing.

"Dude, this is not annotating."

"Dude, yeah it is. And it's not like you were getting anywhere anyway with that—quite shitty, might I mention—drawing of a cactoflowerpus." (Cactus + flower + octopus).

"It's better than your shitty-ass questions," Arizona rolls her eyes.

"They're better than your shitty-ass relationship," Jacob elbows her before spinning on his heels and walking back to the kitchen, leaving Arizona yelling "THAT WAS UNCALLED FOR!" after his very attractive back.

10

CHAPTER 10

Lara wants to go on a double date. She walks into the living room, where Arizona sits on the couch, clad in her Peanuts pajamas and with a bowl of cereal balanced dangerously on a cushion on her lap. Lara, on the other hand, is in an itty bitty pair of shorts and a small t-shirt.

"Go on a double date with us," she says.

"Put on a bra first, and maybe I'll talk to you," Arizona mutters, focusing on the Friends rerun on the television. Sighing, Lara crosses her arms over her chest (which really does not help at all) and leans against the wall.

"Please."

"Why?" Arizona narrows her eyes suspiciously at her older sister.

"Because. I want to spend more time with my sister."

"And you need to go on a double date for that," she deadpans the older girl. "Please, you probably just have a crush on Jeremy, or something."

"I don't have a crush on your boyfriend, Zona. I am very committed to Ross."

Arizona smirks because Ross is also on the television screen, making out with Rachel, and this amuses her. Whoops.

"Can't we just go shopping or whatever, instead," she whines, eyebrows furrowed.

"No. We're going to fancy restaurant tomorrow night. Tell Jeremy. Unless he's not really your boyfriend," she raises her eyebrow at Zona, who glares back.

"Go fuck Ross, or something," she shoots back, shoving a spoon of cereal into her mouth and turning back to the screen.

"I will!" she says indignantly from the hall.

"Good!"

"Good!"

Jeremy won't be at The Number, today, and Arizona tries her best to clamp her fluttering heart's wings down. As she enters the café, the bell hanging from the door's handle jingles, announcing her arrival. Jacob is behind the coffee machine at the counter, hair messy (and definitely not in the sexy way), black apron tied around his waist. His gray shirt clings deliciously to his chest and shit, Arizona needs to get a hold of herself. Clearing her throat and blinking a few times, she walks towards him and takes a seat in one of the spinning stools across from him. She says in an attempt at being casual, "Hey, Jacob."

Said boy's eyes snap up immediately and a slow grin slides onto his lips. "Hey, Arizona May. Didn't know you had a shift today?" He presses down on a lever.

"Don't. I just need to ask you something."

"What?" Jacob asks in a half-detached tone, eyelids lowered to whatever he is doing, and his eyelashes brush his cheeks, they're so long.

Arizona bites her lip and smiles hopefully. "A favor...?"

"And why?" He drags out the y, scratching his head.

"Because of my sister."

"I like your sister," he says in a conversational tone, pouring coffee into some mugs. "She's hot."

She rolls her eyes. "That's great. So you're willing to go on a double date with her and her boyfriend?"

"What?" his eyes swiftly cut to hers, nearly spilling some of the coffee onto his hand. Cursing, he jumps back, wiping the drink off the counter with a towel.

"She wants to have "sister bonding time" and shit, and thinks that going on a double date is the best idea ever," Arizona rolls her eyes again, grabbing the mugs to put on a tray, which she balances on her palm. "What table?"

"Two. Thanks."

Nodding, she slides off the stool to serve the coffee to the diners, before walking back behind the counter to lean against it next to him.

"And," she continues, "if you remember, that one time she met "Jeremy, my boyfriend," you were Jeremy, my boyfriend."

"Oh, yeah. You owe me for that, too. You know, it's never a good idea to owe a lot of things, people get shot for that."

"Sure, whatever. And I'll owe you for this, too. Please. Only for tomorrow night," she clasps her hands under her chin in what she hopes an adorable way. Jacob sighs and leans against the counter to survey her wearily. He runs a hand through his black hair, pushing it back from his eyes.

"Fine, whatever. You have to do whatever I ask, though," he tells her in warning tone, and she grins, winding her arms around his shoulders in a very brief hug before drawing back and patting his chest. He looks slightly amused at her now-flustered face as she clears her throat and dusts some imaginary lint off his shoulder before patting him again.

"You're the best."

"I know. Now help me."

"So, I guess you like reading?" says Ross from Arizona's doorway, hands shoved into his blue jean pockets.

"How'd you guess?" Arizona asks, grinning, glancing over her shoulder at hime. He smiles back, leaning forward to peer his head into her room, eyes skipping from pile of books to pile of books, over the Friends and the V for Vendetta posters.

"Lara sent me to see if you're ready."

"Yeah, just one sec. And we need to pick up Ja—Jeremy, if that's alright," she stumbles over her words, shoving her phone charger and The Half-Blood Prince into her bag.

"Hey, why do you always do that?" Ross asks and she blinks at him probably a million times, face flushing.

"W—what?" Arizona feigns innocence and his eyebrows raise as he leans against the doorjamb.

"JaJeremy. You never say Jeremy, it's always JaJeremy, as if you forgot his name or something."

Holy shit, this cannot be happening. Not Ross, Lara's boyfriend of all people. Nonononono.

"What, uh, what are you talking about? Why would I ever forget my boyfriend's name?" Her laugh is so fake she nearly cringes.

"Don't tell me then," Ross smirks, "but there's something weird going on here. And if you don't want anyone figuring it out, I'd recommend that you try harder to hide it." And with that, he turns on his heels and walks up the basement stairs leaving Arizona standing in the middle of her carpeted floor, chest pounding so loudly that it echoes in her bedroom.

After a few more seconds of complete shock and, okay, maybe a little terror, Arizona shakes her head, hoists her bag over her head to cross over her body. She sighs to settle her rattling heart and turns off the lights on her way upstairs. Lara is standing in Ross's arms, smile huge and gorgeous, as he says something to her and when she leans up to kiss him, Arizona groans loudly and walks out the door, muttering about how disgusting they are.

Like a true Oregonian, Ross drives a Prius hybrid, and scowling, she sits down in the back seat. Arizona does not want to go on a double date with her sister. When Ross asks for directions, she grudgingly tells him how to get to the Millers'. When they pull into their driveway, Arizona doesn't budge, and Lara twists in her seat to poke her knee.

"Go get your boyfriend."

"You go get my boyfriend," Arizona grumbles, climbing out of her seat and shutting the door noisily, "you seem to appreciate him more than me, anyway."

Earlier today, Jacob had informed her that nobody would be home, so she remembers to press on the doorbell a few extra seconds, making sure that the buzzing is definitely heard by him. Sure enough, he opens the door with a peeved expression, and Arizona does her best to concentrate on that instead of how fucking good he looks tonight.

"Ready?" she asks with an overly excited grin and rolling his eyes, he steps out, locking the door behind him. Jacob had traded his t-shirt for a dark blue button-down and a black jacket. Arizona can't deny that he looks incredible, so she swivels around and marches back to the car, not waiting for him. A moment after getting in, he sits down in the seat next to hers.

"Hey, Jeremy," says Lara with her stupid sultry voice and after blinking, Jacob smiles that same slow, easy smile.

"Hey," he replies and Ross grins, shaking his head at Jacob's just as flirty voice, before starting the car again and backing out of the driveway.

Halfway through the ride, as Ross and Lara talk amongst themselves, Jacob leans over so close that Arizona can feel his breathe against her ear. She bites her lip hard and tries to not give anything away. But that's okay, because her freaking blush does it for her, anyway. And then he whispers, "Your sister looks hot."

"Dude!" Arizona whisper-yells and he laughs, leaning back again, he pats her leg comfortingly.

"It's okay, Arizona May, you're still hotter."

Said girl's mouth hangs open as she stares at him with wide eyes, as he laughs silently, shaking his head.

"Dude!"

Jacob returns from the buffet for probably the third time that night, collapsing into his chair happily, plate before him, fork in hand, eyebrows wiggling. "Man, pretending to be your boyfriend is fun," he grins at Arizona from across the table, and she kicks him lightly on the shin. Jacob pulls an apalled look and she rolls her eyes.

"You're paying, y'know."

"We're splitting."

"Oh. Okay, fine."

"I was kidding," he blinks, shoving noodles into his mouth. "I'm definitely paying."

"No, we're splitting," Arizona shakes her head rapidly and leans back into her chair, arms crossed over her chest. Lara and Ross had gone to get some soft serve ice-cream from the machine in the back of the room, and the last time Arizona had turned to look at them, Ross was really struggling with it. Jacob sets his fork back down onto the plate with a clatter and leans forward on his forearms crossed on the table, eyebrows raised in amusement.

"Has anyone ever told you that you're a really freaking fickle person?"

"Yes."

"I mean, you know, I've always been really attracted to the stubborn, sexy girls, but I dunno, I'm kinda digging this can't-make-up-her-mind thing." Arizona narrows her eyes at him and he grins cheekily. "Kidding, calm down. But, I'm paying, Arizona May, now shut up and eat your whatever the hell that is."

"It's tomato basil soup."

"Oh. Right. That." He leans over to peer into her bowl and she does her best to ignore how cute he looks like that. "That looks really good, actually. Are you really going to eat all that? You look really full, if you ask me."

"Are you calling me fat?" Arizon grins and his eyes get big.

"No! I'm not—you're not—you're p—"

Arizona laughs and he frowns, until she sighs and slides her bowl over to him, and his grin spreads at record speed.

"Man, my brother got lucky—to get such a great sister-in-law!" he finishes quickly as Lara and Ross show up suddenly, and he nearly chokes on how much soup he pours into his mouth. Trying not to laugh, Arizona meets the other two's gaze. Lara obliviously slips into her chair, tiny cone of vanilla in her hand. Ross, on the other hand, sits down slowly, eyes flicking from Arizona to Jacob, and back again. Swallowing, Arizona raises her brows at him in an innocent manner, and Ross shakes his head slightly.

"So, Jeremy," Lara licks her cone and Jacob bites back a smile, "how did you Zona end up with someone like you?" Arizona makes a mocking face at the girl next to her and Jacob grins. And then Arizona realizes that everybody knows "Jeremy" is not in high school anymore, and she and Jacob had never really quite worked out the details about their story. Jacob seems to realize this at the same time and his eyes widen momentarily before blinking and pasting on that charming grin.

"Well, actually, we met at The Number."

Oh? Arizona thinks.

"Oh?" says Lara.

"Yeah, she was, uh, she ordered a coffee. And it was raining that day. And I remember coming out of the kitchen, and she was on the other side of the room, drinking coffee and reading a book." Arizona sinks low in her seat and presses a fist to her mouth, stifling any laughter that is threatening to spill out at the incredible cheesiness falling from Jacob's mouth right now. "And I just thought she was the prettiest girl ever—she is the prettiest girl ever." he smiles at Arizona, who flushes despite herself, and with a wink Jacob turns back to the other two. "So I put my number on her cup and probably quoted some cheesy song, but apparently she liked it, so here we are. Thank God, she's nearly almost eighteen, am I right?"

Arizona ducks down to choke down her chortles and Jacob kicks her under the table. She kicks him back. When she rises again, he wiggles his eyebrows at her, grin blinding and cocky. It's kind of disgusting how good he looks. And it's even more disgusting that this is Arizona's boyfriend's older brother, goddammit.

11

——— • ———

CHAPTER 11

Crosley heaves yet another angsty sigh, flopping over onto the couch and dangling his ridiculously long leg off the side. His head lands on the binder resting in Arizona's lap and his brown hair flips into his eyes. Groaning, he rubs his head but doesn't move from where he is.

"You know," Arizona says, shifting to accommodate him and herself, "usually people move when they're in an uncomfortable position."

"No, don't move," Crosley protests tiredly, eyes shut. She can see a tiny bit of stubble on his chin and rolls her eyes.

"I'm talking about you, dumbass. Also, do my eyes deceive me or are you finally starting to grow facial hair?"

Crosley's eyes open and narrow at her, but she's looking at him upside down so she can't really tell. "Shut up. I've had facial hair since freshman year, I just shaved so you could never tell."

"Please," Arizona mutters, tucking hair behind her ear and leaning closer to the textbook next to her to read the problem. "You had no sense of personal hygeine freshman year, if you got facial hair then, I would have noticed because shaving it would be the last thing on your list."

"Hey!" At this he sits up, pushing her roughly to the side, and he settles back down into a tiny ball, feet smooshed up against Arizona's thigh. "I did too have personal hygeine. I got all the girls, remember?"

"Hah. You did not, for both of those. And then Gem came and it all changed," Arizona says dramatically and he jerks his foot suddenly, kicking her so that her pencil flies out of her fingers. "Dude! Why are you even here? Yours is the house with all the food, anyway, remember?"

"I like your couch," he mumbles, curling his face into a pillow, and Arizona smirks.

"Wanna know what I think?"

"Mm."

"You missed me. You wanted to talk to me, so you came over."

"What if I did?"

"Awww," Arizona cooes, laughing, leaning over to squeeze his cheeks and yelping, he shoves her off, kicking her so hard that this time she falls off the couch. "Holy shit, man, ow?"

"Don't do that," Crosley frowns, resting his head sideways on his forearm as he looks at her.

"You're the one that missed me, you cutie patootie," Arizona reaches for his cheeks again and he flicks his tongue out, nearly licking her finger. She recoils in disgust. "Seriously though, how does Gem like you?"

"She does not."

"Uh, dude, yeah she does. Besides, we still have that deal."

"Yeah, and you have to break up with Jeremy first."

Pursing her lips, Arizona shuts the textbook and her notebook, shoving the hair out of her eyes. She leans back against the couch and Crosley turns to look at her, grin slow and big.

"Wanna watch a movie?"

"Which one?"

"I dunno, hold on." He crawls over to the shelf of DVDs beside the television, resting on his knees as he looks through them. Sitting back on the balls of his feet, he flicks a couple of movies up, over his shoulder. "The Lion King or Submarine?"

"Let's watch Submarine, I love that one."

"The Lion King it is, then."

"Dick."

"Okay," he clears his throat, sliding the CD in and standing up to reach for the home phone. "You make the popcorn, I'll call everyone."

"Everyone as in Gem?"

"You wanna go, you little shit?"

There are two new kids at the rehabilitation: a pale girl with black hair who apparently goes by Cesca, and a boy with eyes bluer than Jacob's, by the name of Evan. Sunday, the head of the center had told Arizona to introduce the two to the rest of the Team Circle. Arizona leads a group discussion once a month, where all the kids (plus Webby, who actually should not even be there) talk to each other about their lives and how it's all been going. It's basically a group therpy session.

"We have two newcomers today, Cesca and Evan," she says now, grinning at the two mentioned. "Everybody be welcoming." Everybody in the circle grumbles a greeting together, and just like everything in this building, it's gray and sarcastic, and Arizona bites back a smile. "I'm Arizona and it's awesome to have you two here," Arizona bobs her head at them, and Cesca's eyes are so black it's kind of a little scary, so Arizona turns away, just as James leans over to whisper something in Cesca's ear.

"Now," Arizona May starts again, hands on hips, lips pursed as she surveys them. "Who has something they'd like to share? Accomplishment. Story. Needed advice." Nobody raises their hands and sighing, she collapses into ane mpty chair next to James. Valencia, a tall girl with crazy black curls, tentatively raises her hand, and Arizona grins, nodding. "Valencia! Yes!"

"I, um, used the internet today."

Valencia is a bit of an old soul, and Arizona smiles.

"Oh? And how did that go—"

"Arizona May!" a different voice calls from the other side of the room, and automatically, everybody's heads turn to find the source. Arizona turns last, and slowest, because she already knows who it is. Jacob stands in the doorjamb, clad in a blue t-shirt that does nothing but make his eyes look even prettier, and khakis. Arizona doesn't know what her face looks like at the moment, but judging from everybody else's terrified looks and Jacob's smug one, she probably looks very scary. When angry, Arizona's eyebrows tend to lower so far that her eyes almost disappear. Somewhere in the background she hears Adeeb yell a hah!

Jeremy or Lara have been picking Arizona up for the last few weeks, and neither of the two are here right now, and Arizona doesn't think it's healthy for her to be seeing so much of her boyfriend's older brother.

"I told you he would come today! They are so sleeping with each other," says Adeeb to James and Arizona physically restrains herself from kicking his ass. "Oh," he starts explaining to Evan and Cesca, ignoring Arizona's death glare. "This guy is like, always visiting Arizona May, and apparently he's an ass or whatever, and she hates him, but we all know that it's bullshit and they're having an affair. James and me—"

"James and I," James mumbles.

"have this bet going on about whether they are having an affair or not and every time I say he's coming and James says that he's not, or vice v ersa, we bet Damaged Dimes on it." Shaking her head, Arizona glares and stands up, grudgingly heading to where Jacob straightens up from the wall he had been leaning against.

"How's it going, Arizona May?"

"What are you doing here?" Arizona rolls her eyes and his half-smile stretches into a full one.

"Picking you up."

"Again?"

"Again. Not my fault my brother's kinda a douchebag."

"Dude, don't say that!" Arizona thwacks his shoulder and he laughs a little bit.

"Also, is there a reason for why four people are staring straight at us?"

Turning around, Arizona, quite predictably, finds Adeeb, James, Cesca, and Evan watching their every move, and grinning, she turns back around and raises her brows at the amused boy.

"No, not at all. I just complain about you sometimes."

"Cute. Anyway, I'm going to be waiting in the car, so hurry up, yeah?"

Without receiving a response (only because he doesn't wait for one), Jacob swivels on his heels and marches out of the Activities

Room, and then down the staircase, (beautifully) broad shoulders disappearing from Arizona's sight after a moment.

And them Arizona hurries back to the circle, where everybody pretends to be consumed in their own conversations, and smiles at Valencia. "Tell us what happened," she insists, but everyone, including Valencia, is smirking at her. "Shut up,"Arizona snaps at them, but they all just laugh and make innocent faces. "I hate him," she cries and slumps back down in the chair, and then everybody is surrounding her, comforting her, teasing her.

"This happens a lot, too," Adeeb says to Evan and Cesca in what he thinks is a low voice, but not really, because Arizona can hear him loud and clear. She kicks him in the ankle and he kicks her back without even looking. "We talk about and to her more than we do with each other. It's quite fun, actually."

"'Kay, you know what, you guys are good, go ahead," Arizona narrows her eyes and gestures to the door, more specifically at Adeeb. He only smirks and high-fives one of her extended hands.

"Sorry 'bout that," mutters James as he passes by, and Arizona smiles. James is the only genuinely kind person in here.

Alex comes to The Number that afternoon, and he brings the sun in with his presence as he enters the café. "Arizona!" he says just like every other time, setting his book down on the counter before sitting himself onto one of the spinny stools before her.

"Hey, Alex."

"Why do you have an apron, and why are you behind the counter?"

"I work here."

"Oh, man, that is awesome! When the hell did this happen?"

"Shit, I dunno, for maybe a couple months?"

"Makin' some extra cash?"

"Yep. Can I get you anything?"

"Please, Arizona, you know what I want."

"I forgot, actually. Sorry, Alex."

"Oh. Black coffee and chocolate biscotti." Alex laughs and shakes his head before folding his arms on the tabletop and leaning forward. "So ho—"

That's when Jeremy chooses to amble out of the kitchen, apron tied around his neck and what looks to be flour on his forehead. He spots Arizona and that killer smile takes over his lips. "Hey!" he says, untying the apron and hanging it up before hugging her and grabbing a mug.

"Hi! Are you done with your shift?"

"I'm on break," he explains, before looking at Alex.

"Oh, this is Alex, my...mom's ex."

"Oh." Jeremy's eyebrows rise adorably and he blinks a few times before offering a hand, which Alex shakes while sneaking a few suggestive looks at Arizona, who only rolls them away with her eyes.

"This is Jeremy, my boyfriend."

Arizona still isn't used to that word on her tongue. Boyfriend, boyfriend, boyfriend.

"Oh, so you're Jeremy. Wow, Arizona, you've got good taste, I must say." Alex winks and Arizona leans over to shove his elbow off the counter. He nearly topples over the stool. Turning to Jeremy, Arizona reaches up to brush the flour away from his forehead, and his smile is warm.

"You, uh, you had flour. On your face."

"Yeah, I figured as much when you brushed flour off my face," Jeremy grins and Arizona laughs.

"You guys are cute," says Alex and Jeremy nudges Arizona, wiggling his eyebrows.

"I know."

Arizona feels a little bit woozy. Freaking Jeremy smiles.

12

—·—

CHAPTER 12

Arizona hadn't remembered about the party until Jeremy knocked on her door. She is in her Peanuts pajamas as she opens the door, and there her boyfriend stands, eyebrows raised as he scans her in amusement.

The one Jeremy had invited her a few weeks ago was pushed back along with his parents' trip, and he decided to throw it right after finals ended, on a warm Friday night.

"I see that you're ready," he states with his killer grin and she blinks multiple times before the realization dawns on her, and she collapses against the wall, cursing.

"Shit, I forgot about that! I'm so sorry, I'll go get ready right now. Come in."

The last she sees of Jeremy as she sprints down the stairs to her room, is him ambling around in a tiny circle near the door. He looks adorably awkward and there's something nagging at the back of her head, about how something isn't right, but she pays no mind to it, because all she cares about right now is changing so fast that she gets a medal.

Quickly, she throws on the first dress (of the three she has) in her closet, and braids her hair to the side, tying it off with an elastic and running back up to the kitchen. Arizona grabs her set of housekeys from the key dish and when she turns, she sees Lara leaning against the counter, apple in hand, mid-bite.

"Tell Mom I'm going," she tells the older girl, whose face is questioning. Arizona doesn't have time for this shit. So, spinning on her heels, she starts to walk briskly out of the kitchen. She is almost out, when Lara speaks up from behind.

"Who's the cute guy out front?"

Arizona stops, internally screaming. Fuck. She saw Jeremy, who she doesn't know is Jeremy, because she thinks that Jacob is Jeremy.

"Uh, he's Jeremy's brother. I have to go to some party at their house, and he's picking me up," she blurts out, and just then, the boy in question' head pops up from around the corner.

"Arizona? Are you ready? You look great, by the way," he grins, and then sees Lara. His eyebrows rise visibly, because it seems as if every straight boy is attracted to her, and then he steps out with his hand risen, ready for a handshake. "Hi—"

"Yep, I'm ready, let's go. Don't wanna be late," Arizona grins nervously, grabbing the raised hand and pulling Jeremy out of the kitchen, down the hall, and out the door. "Bye, Lara!" Arizona calls, not waiting for a response before shutting it behind her.

"That your sister?" he asks, as they walk to the car.

"Mhm. Lara."

"Oh. She's nice."

"Nice as in hot?" she asks with a smirk and he flushes.

"No—I mean—"

"It's okay," Arizona laughs, too amused by his antics to be annoyed. "I'm used to it."

"Not that you're not," he continues, flustered and Arizona decides to stay quiet to see what he has to say. "I mean, you're very pretty." Ah, there it is. Lara is hot, Lara is sexy. Arizona's cute, she's pretty.

This time, Arizona is a bit peeved, but then she remembers that she spends way too much time with this boy's older brother, which is kind of really unhealthy, so she pastes a smile onto her lips and laughs. "It's okay, Jeremy, it's fine."

"Really?"

"Really."

Arizona's never been to a high school party before. Hell, she wasn't even aware that there were kids at her school that threw high school parties. She's only ever read about them in teen fiction novels, and usually, the female protagonist ends up drunk off her ass via keg stand. Arizona's not very comfortable with getting drunk off her ass via keg stand, so she is wary when entering the house with Jeremy.

"Want a drink?" Jeremy yells over the ground-shaking music.

"Coke is fine," Arizona smiles and with a nod, he turns to disappear into the crowd. Only a second later does she realize her mistake and wishes that she had gone with Jeremy, because God knows when he'll be back.

As if on cue, a certain tall boy with certain black hair and certain blue eyes appears next to Arizona.

"What're you doing here, Arizona May?"

Jacob grins down at her and she widens her eyes at him, "Partying, duh."

"Right." He glances down at her dress. "Right. You're having lots of fun, yeah?"

"You know what," she rolls her eyes and crosses her arms, watching the blob of people dancing in the middle of the living room, or as close to dancing as they can get at the ridiculously intoxicated state they are all in. Everyone else mostly stands around the edge, talking, and there's a number of couples getting hot and heavy in corners. "Do you have the wifi password?"

"Nope, sorry."

Staring at Jacob with huge eyes, Arizona's mouth drops. "Are you serious? You don't know the wifi password?"

He grins, laughing a little. "No, I do, I just wanted to see how you'd react if I didn't. Hey, Arizona May, did you know that you're pathetic?"

Punching him in the arm lightly, Arizona hands him her phone, and he taps at it, taking longer than Arizona expects. "Nice nudes," he mutters, and Arizona yelps, grabbing at the phone and clicking it off before shoving it into her pocket. Only after this does she realize that she doesn't have any nudes. Chuckling, Jacob shakes his head before looking at her again. "Wait, does that mean you actually do have nudes on there, then? Because—" He reaches for her phone again and smacking his hand away, Arizona frowns.

"No, I don't have n—!"

"Here's your Coke." Jeremy's back, handing a red Solo cup to Arizona. Thanking him, she sips once at the drink and then promptly chokes and makes a face as it burns its way down her throat.

"That's not Coke, Jeremy."

"Oh, crap, wrong cup, sorry!"

Trading her cup for the one in his hand, he smiles apologetically at her and she laughs. "No, it's fine." Arizona makes sure to smell it first before drinking it this time, and thankfully, it actually is Coke this time.

"Wow," says Jacob in a mock enthusiastic tone, looking from Jeremy to Arizona, "you guys are practically kissing right now!"

"Don't you have some girl to bother?" Arizona scowls at him over the rim of the cup and he winks, smile cheeky.

"Yes, and I'm doing that right now."

"Dude, my girlfriend," Jeremy sighs, not even that bothered by Jacob's blatant—not to mention totally uncalled for—flirting.

"Shut up and drink your disgusting beer, child," says Jacob.

"What kind of a shit sentence is that, anyway?" Arizona asks, arms outstretched, palms facing up.

"The best kind."

"Go away, Jacob."

"Okay."

It is halfway through the night, when Romy makes her presence obvious to Arizona. She comes stumbling to the left arm of the couch, on which Arizona perches, thumb scrolling through her phone.

"Zona, sup, my bitcherella." Romy, flops down next to her friend.

"Romy! Where in hell did you just come from?"

"The bedroom."

Immediately, Arizona's eyes widen and her eyebrows rise. "Yo, who's the lucky guy, man?"

"The bed."

"Oh."

"I was taking a nap, Zona."

"Oh."

"Yeah."

The two girls lean back into the couch, watching the party that hasn't thinned out even the slightest bit since the start. "So, what're you doing here?" asks Arizona and Romy shrugs, head tilting back to rest on the pillow.

"I heard about the party, so I came."

"Alone?"

"Actually, no," Romy seems to realize that she has lost the people she has come with, and she stands up, face panicked. "Crosley and Gem came, too."

"Ah. And did you think you wouldn't be third-wheeling or something? Or that they wouldn't leave you by your lonesome self as they went to the nearest bedroom to do God knows what?"

"Actually, they said they wanted to come, and I asked if those things you just listed would happen, and Crosley walked away and Gem slapped my arm, so I just took that as a no. But now that I think about it, they never said they wouldn't. Dammit!"

"Best not to bother them," Arizona tugs Romy back down and sighs. "Who knows what base they're at now."

Jeremy had left a few minutes back with a group of his friends, and Arizona hadn't really minded at all. She's seen all those very dependent couples at school, the ones in which one half, or just both halves, can't survive a single minute without the other, and it kind of exhausts Arizona just watching them. She likes to believe that her not minding Jeremy leaving her temporarily is a good thing. She likes to think that this is a very healthy relationship. Arizona really does like to think so.

13

CHAPTER 13

Arizona has never seen so much royal blue in her entire life.

The sun is blinding in her eyes, and reaching out, she grabs Crosley to position him before her, and he is just tall enough to block the light. "Thanks, man." Crosley grunts in response, eyes glued to the phone in his hand. Arizona rolls her own pair and turns to Romy, who is grinning so largely that Arizona nearly winces. Romy flicks her blonde fringe out of her eyes and blinks at Arizona.

"Dude. We're done with public education. Forever."

"Can't wait to get out of this hellhole," Gem mutters from beside Romy, just as Briana bounds up to her friends, Christine in tow.

"Congrats, you guys!" Briana yells and tugs everybody down to her height for a hug. Crosley sighs, shoves his phone back into his pocket, and obliges. "Christine's here."

"We can see that," Crosley raises his eyebrows, and Arizona slaps his bicep. He frowns at his arm before knocking it into Arizona's stomach, with a lot of force. "Oops."

"Fuckin' dick."

"Good to know, Zonie."

"What the fuck did you just call me?"

"You know exac-"

Arizona slams her foot down on Crosley's, and yelping a very high-pitched yelp, he scowls at her and grabs at his foot. Crosley growls and moves to stand next to Gem, away from Arizona, who only smirks.

"You guys seem excited," Christine says, fixing the red beret over her pin-straight black hair.

"Okay, Christine, now is not the time for your whole I'm-older-and-I-can-give-you-children-life-advice." Gem crosses her arms and Christine grins and raises her hands.

"It was a fair question."

"Don't mind Gem, she's just bitter over not getting into every single Ivy League school." Crosley rolls his eyes and Gem sticks her tongue out at the grinning boy.

"You can leave, Cros," says Arizona. "You know, hang out with some guys for the first time since first grade. Just a suggestion. You do know that we all think of you as 'one of the girls,' right?"

"Excuse you, I have friends that are boys."

"I'm sure you do," says Christine and Crosley makes a sound of protest.

"I've spoken to you about three times in my entire life, you have no right," he says to Christine, who giggles.

"Shut up, Crosley."

"Yes, please do."

"You're a loser, Cros."

The actual ceremony, in and of itself, had been quite a long, boring process. Georgie Cortez, the valedictorian, had given her speech, at which Briana had teared up, much to her friends' amusement. ("Briana, are you crying?" "No, shut up, Christine." "Awww, Bri-ana." "I hate you.")

Now they stand in the plaza. The night has cooled down with a comfortable breeze and the pink skies are sufficiently sinking into dark blue ones, much like the robes hanging off of everybody's shoulders. Christine, appointed for the duty of picture-taking, rarely stands still, running around to get different angles and shots of the-holy shit-graduates.

Crosley is sad over having lost his hat somewhere inside the hall, and Gem keeps telling him to "holy crap, Crosley, build a bridge and get over it." A flash erupts from the camera in front of Arizona and she blinks, jutting her head back with a start. This leads to her accidentally head-butting Romy ("Son of a fucking bitch, holy fucking hell!"), and exasperated, Briana steals the camera from Christine ("Gimme that.")

"Zona, hun'!" Cora's blonde hair is bright in the dark, almost as much as her huge grin. "Congratulations! How does it feeel?"

Not waiting for an answer, she gathers the girl to her chest in a big hug, and when she lets Arizona go, her father, Lara, and Ross appear. Looking around, Arizona finds everybody else with their parents, save for Christine, who has somehow gotten a hold of the camera, again.

"Here," Ross tilts a little envelope into Arizona's hand before wrapping an arm around Lara, whose smile-for once-looks genuinely genuine. Ripping it open, a giftcard to Candies, the online store.

"Wow, thanks, you guys!" Smiling, she hugs the couple. And as weird as it is to say, it's more awkward with Lara than it is with Ross. "So, my friends and I were gonna go out to dinner, so..."

"You said so twice," mutters Crosley, and Arizona elbows him without looking, and she smirks when she hears his "my boob!"

"Oh, oh yeah that's fine!" Cora grins, so excited that it's doubtful that she'll say no to anything in this moment. Arizona is half tempted to ask if she can get a tattoo. "Congrats, you guys!" A second later, Arizona's family is gone.

"Arizona!"

The mentioned girl turns to find no other than Jeremy dodging hats and robes to get to them, 100-watt killer smile on.

"Hey! Congrats!" Arizona hugs him and his smile doesn't let up.

"Thanks, you do-I still can't believe that it's all over, you know."

"Jhyeah, I can. It's about time," Romy grumbles.

Eventually the five teens plus Christine stumble out of the suffocating crowd of hats and robes, and split into two cars. Jeremy had invited them all to The Number for a free dinner, upon the request of Mrs. Miller.

At the moment Gem and Crosley argue over the radio station, Gem doing her best to switch it to hers while keeping the eye on the road. "Come on, Gem-Crash and Burn sucks! Switch it back." Sighing, Arizona flops an arm over her eyes. Their little fights had been cute at first, but now they were never endless, and it kind of scared Arizona to think of just how worse they'll become once the two get together-which, by the way, is inevitable.

"Nope."

"Gem."

"No."

"Gem, please."

"No."

"I will love you forever, Gem."

"Do you not, already, dickhead?"

Arizona snorts from the back seat, "Believe me, he does."

"Shut the fuck up, Zona," says Crosley.

"My car, my rules, Crosley."

"Gemmmm."

"Cry me a river, asswipe."

"That's a good song," says Crosley, finally letting up and crossing his arms as he relaxes back into the passenger's seat. Arizona hums in agreement.

When they finally arrive at the restaurant, The Number is already packed with other classmates that opted out of getting drunk on graduation night. Romy marches in and slides into a booth at the very back of the room, Arizona sitting down next to her, followed by the rest of the group. While Crosley and Gem bicker a bit more and Briana and Christine giggle about something and Romy stares intensely at the menu, Arizona lets her eyes roam the rest of the small café.

She spots Georgie Cortez with some of her friends, and she is currently bright pink in the face as she speaks to the waiter. Said waiter turns around suddenly and Arizona realizes why Georgie Cortez had resembled a tomato. Jacob meets her eyes and a slow, steady, dangerously sexy smiles slides onto his lips before he saunters over to their table.

"Congratulations, Arizona May." At his voice the rest of the table looks up and his eyes flit over their faces before he adds on as an afterthought, "...and company."

"Thanks."

"So, how does it feel?" He raises his eyebrows and pulls a nearby chair over to sit on it backwards.

"Why does everybody keep asking me that, it doesn't feel much different," Arizona rolls his eyes and he shrugs. "And shouldn't you be waiting on people like every other good paid waiter?"

"Probably."

"I'm not tipping you, you know. You're a horrible waiter."

Romy scoffs and mumbles in a low voice, "I am, because I mean fuck me now."

"I'm pretty sure he heard that," says Arizona and Jacob laughs a little.

"And what's your name?" he asks in a charming voice, grinning disarmingly at Romy, who looks conflicted. Probably deciding on whether she should pass out or jump the gorgeous boy in front of her.

"He totally heard you," says Arizona, sighing. "This is Romy. That's Gem, Crosley, Briana, and Christine. This is Jacob, Jeremy's older brother."

Crosley's mouth shapes a little o, which then widens to a smirk a split-second later, Briana's smiling politely, Romy is biting her lip, Christine coughs, and Gem's eyebrows are risen. "You guys ready to order?" asks Jacob and immediately everybody recovers, clearing their throats and nodding. Taking their orders swiftly, he turns on his heels to walk back to the register, and Romy isn't inconspicuous when checking out his butt.

"That is one sweet ass."

Arizona stares at Romy.

"And now I see why dating Jeremy is such a problem, because fucking hell."

"He does have a very cute butt," Briana nods, and when Christine elbows her, she elbows Christine back.

"Right here, Briana, your girlfriend is right here," says Christine, not without fondness.

"Hush, I still love you, it's okay."

"I have a cute butt too, you know."

"Oh, I know, Christine. I know."

"Ugh gross, you guys."

"Shut up, Crosley."

Jeremy joins Arizona and her friends later into the night. He had been with his own friends for the first half of the night, and when he comes to The Number, he brings one of the guys Arizona always sees him hanging out with.

"Hey," Jeremy grins and slides in next to Arizona. "This is Isaac."

Isaac is terribly beautiful, with inky hair and eyes the color of rain clouds. His smile is adorably crooked and Romy leans in, suddenly very interested-more, it seems, than she had been with Jacob.

"Isaac has a girlfriend," says Jeremy, who, apparently, also sees the not-very-sneaky Romy. "With whom he is very whipped. Fun fact, he also has an ex that turned out gay."

Crosley snorts loudly and suddenly, and Isaac shrugs, smiling slightly.

"I don't think you have any right to snort," says Arizona to Crosley, who visibly braces himself for the insult that will, no doubt, be shot at him in the next second, "Mr. I-Think-I-Will-Win-The-Heart-Of-My-Life-Long-Crush-By-Fighting-With-Her-Every-Other-Second."

"I'm leaving," says Crosley before unelegantly scooting out of the booth and grabbing a mint.

Romy frowns, "Boo, you whore."

"Oh, but remember, Romy?" says Briana. "Crosley hasn't even watched Mean Girls before."

"What the fuck, Cros," says Romy.

"You deserve to leave," says Christine.

"Actually," says Arizona with a smirk, "I've made him watch it. And remember when he refused to watch it because he thought it was more chick-flick than comedy? He actually really loved it."

"You promised not to tell!"

14

CHAPTER 14

Fourth of July in downtown Portland is a lovely, loud thing. Every person lines up at the edges of the river, and they come hours early to set up their chairs. And when the lights start, the entire city goes dark and silent, and the only thing that can be heard is the burst of fireworks in the air.

Arizona had gone with her family every year for the two-thirds of her life, and as soon as she had been deemed old enough, she'd go with her friends. Every year, the friends had planned out what would happen, but this year there had been procrastination involved, and now Arizona has no idea what the hell is happening. She taps a message and sends it to Crosley.

R u coming???

Sat @ 4:11 PM

jesus christ, arizona, use whole words

Sat @ 4:17 PM

Just ans me dammit

Sat @ 4:18 PM

how does this feel?

zona zona zona zona zona zona

Sat @ 4:19 PM

StOp

Sat @ 4:19 PM

zOnAAAA

Sat @ 4:20 PM

ans me, u asswipe!!!!

Sat @ 4:25 PM

THAT'S HOW IT FEELS, ZONA

Sat @ 4:27 PM

ur so fuckin annoying omfg ihu

Sat @ 4:28 PM

:(

Sat @ 4:28 PM

fine wtvr ily

Sat @ 4:29 PM

:)

Sat @ 4:29 PM

R U COMING OR NOT?!?!?!?!!?!?!??

Sat @ 4:29 PM

yes i'm coming jeez, calm the fuck down, woman

Sat @ 4:30 PM

zona?

Sat @ 4:31 PM

zona, you there?

Sat @ 4:34 PM

arizona i'm sorry come backkk D:

Sat @ 4:37 PM

ur ugly

Sat @ 4:42 PM

Crosley arrives at Arizona's door half an hour later with Romy and Gem and a cooler filled to the brim with sodas and sparkling waters (for Romy, who is trying a "No-Soda-No-Bullshit" diet).

"We were at The Number and Jeremy was there, so I told him to come," says Gem, and Arizona's eyes widen.

"No!"

"What?"

"I don't want to spend more time with him than I already have to! I told you, I don't like him like that."

"You mean like-like?" gasps Romy. She slaps Arizona on the back before trudging into the house and down the stairs to Arizona's room.

"Do you guys find amusement in watching my "love life" fall apart around me, or something?" Arizona narrows her eyes and makes finger quotation marks when she says love life.

"Yes," says Crosley before following Gem and Romy to the basement. The group had finally worked out what would be happening, and Briana would be coming, and they would all leave Arizona's house in Crosley's car. It's a small, dying thing, and it's been the group's mode of transportation for the past few years, ever since Cros had gotten his license.

As soon as Briana arrives, the teenagers pile into Crosley's tiny Toyota, Romy struggling with the back left-side door that has a tendency to stick unless someone kicks it. It takes Crosley nine tries to get the car to start up, and Arizona sticks her head out of the window several times in order to breathe. There is already the sound of fireworks bursting in air, and by the time they get to downtown, it's six o'clock. Cars line the sidewalks, despite the fact that there is still three hours until the show starts. Crosley finds a parking spot near the science museum, and the group walks a few minutes to get to a decent place. People are just starting to set up their chairs, and a kid in a Cars t-shirt runs past, giggling as he throws little things down on the ground, which create a horribly loud snapping noise. Arizona yelps and jumps out of the way.

"Fuckin' kids," Romy mutters, glaring, as she unfolds her chair, "I hate kids."

"We know," says Gem.

The sun is low and orange, hiding behind the buildings, reflecting in the water of the river. The air smells of smoke and hot dogs, and it's brilliant. "Wanna get a hot dog?" Arizona asks Gem, who nods and grunts as she gets up to walk with other girl. A red and white stand is set up beneath the bridge, and there is a short line leading up to it. Getting behind the next person, Arizona turns to smirk at Gem.

"So, you came with Cros, huh?"

"Yeah," Gem says slowly, suspiciously.

"Did he pick you up first?"

"Yeah…"

Arizona giggles and Gem whacks her arm.

"You are so annoying."

"Okay, but you can't really say that, when you have a crush on Crosley of all people."

"Okay, but you can't really say that when you have a crush on Jeremy's older brother of all people."

"I do not!" Arizona glares at Gem, and turns to look at the line behind her. Her eyes spot a certain dark-haired boy, and yelping, Arizona ducks.

"Dammit, why did you invite Jeremy, again?"

"Um, because he's your boyfriend, and if you don't see that, then you have a serious problem, man. Also, you're the one that said "oh, yeah, sure, of coooourse!" when he asked you to go out with him, and you're the one who's too much of a coward to break up with a boy you obviously do not like in any level above platonic. Jesus Christ, Arizona, grow a pair of lady balls and break up with him if you're so afraid of seeing him. If this is what you're like, then I wouldn't be surprised if he proposed to you and you said, and then came to us literally crying. Arizona, I'm sorry, but you're pathetic." Gem raises her eyebrows at the blonde, whose jaw is hanging open at the moment.

"Shit, you're right."

"I know."

"I'm so dumb."

"I know."

"Thanks for the vote of confidence," Arizona rolls her eyes and Gem shoots two thumbs up at her.

"You know it."

Sighing to hold herself together with one breath, Arizona turns to wave at the boy she had been cowering from just a second ago. "Jeremy!" His head whips up and he looks around before spotting her. "Jeremy, hey!" He's with that Isaac boy, again, and another pretty girl with crazy curly, black hair. Arizona waves him over, and he nods cutting ahead of a few people, who protest. Arizona narrows her eyes at them, muttering that she had been saving a spot, and they sigh, rolling their eyes and turning away.

"Hey, Arizona, Happy Fourth of July."

"Yeah. America!"

Arizona sees Gem snort and then grasp at her throat, wincing. That was so bad, she mouths at Arizona, who flips her off with much subtlety.

"That was lame," laughs Jeremy, face incredibly amused.

Arizona giggles, "I know, sorry about that."

"You're cute."

"Oh."

Arizona's face is no doubt pink at the moment, and she can hear Gem's audible sigh. How in hell is Arizona supposed to break up with an adorable boy like this?

Jeremy laughs again, shaking her head before looking back at Isaac and the girl. "You know Isaac, this is Vinnie, his girlfriend. This is Arizona and Gem, right?"

"Yeah," Gem grins briefly, running a hand through her hair and tucking it into her pocket, stance a bit impatient.

"Hi," Arizona waves a little at the other two, who grin back at her. Isaac is really, really pretty, and also has a serious case of the girlfriend, judging from the look clouding his face whenever he glances at Vinnie. Arizona wonders what it feels like to be looked at like that.

Buying their hot dogs, Arizona and Gem, who had asked if Jeremy wanted to join them at their spot and who had also ignored Arizona's death glare, wait for the other three to finish, before leading them to where Crosley is sat on the ground, reading a book Arizona had lent him. Hearing them approach, he glances up, eyes hopeful.

"Did you get me the hot dog?"

"Yeah, here," Arizona hands him the one in her left hand, and sits down next to Romy, who is looking at the meat with a hint of disgust.

"Okay," says Crosley with a fierce glare, "just because you decided to keep yourself from experiencing one of the best parts of life does not mean you get to do the same thing to me." Indignantly, he stuffs half of the hot dog in his mouth, chewing with a point to make, and Arizona groans, pushing his face away.

"That's disgusting, Crosley."

"You're disgusting!" he retorts, but due to the fact that he can't form any words because of the food in his mouth, it comes out more as a "Yow dithguthtinh." Swallowing, he looks up, and his eyes widen. "Oh, hey Jeremy."

"Hey, man." Grinning, he sits down next to Arizona, face alight with bemusement, Isaac and Vinnie on the other side, conversing with one another in quiet voices. They're so adorable it almost makes Arizona sick to look at. She really needs to break up with Jeremy. She wants what they have, what Gem and Crosley have. She wants freaking chemistry, is that really so much to ask?

Eventually the black night curtain hangs low and Arizona pulls the sweater tighter around herself. Crosley pulls out the sparklers from somewhere, grin lit by the lighter touching a flame to the sparklers. They erupt into little stars and he hands one to everybody, adorably excited.

"I fucking love sparklers, man."

"We know, Crosley."

The fireworks start, and Arizona can see the lights reflecting off of Jeremy's coffee-colored eyes like mirrors, and biting her lip, she slides her hand into his hand. Caught off guard, he blinks before a languid smile slides onto his lips and squeezes her hand in his. Arizona holds her breath, focusing on her fingers, and whether there are tingles running up her arm or not, like she's heard happens.

Nope.

Nothing.

Nothing.

15

CHAPTER 15

According to Jeremy, every year his parents throw a small barbecue dinner at a beach house they have at the coast. It's mostly just family friends, and the kids are free to invite any of their friends they want. Jeremy inviting Arizona, though, hadn't been much of a choice, because Mrs. Miller had called the girl up, herself, and demanded that she be there.

This barbecue ends up taking place one warm Tuesday night. Jeremy had told Arizona that she could invite whoever she wanted, and she ends up bringing Romy and Crosley—the latter roped into this with threats to set Gem up with a hot boy Romy knows, because he is the one with the car. The drive to the beach is a long one, filled with multiple (now crushed) cans of sodas (and lemonade for Romy), and lazy conversations, and yes, maybe a few Hot or Not rounds and karaoke sessions.

The second the three step out of Crosley's car, the boy whacks his face, muttering obscenities. "Fuckin' fireflies, who ever said they were pretty was high as a kite." There aren't many fireflies in Oregon, but there are tonight. They flicker like tiny, moving stars in the trees, and the skies are pink, slowly sinking to obscurity behind the rocks Arizona can see waves crashing against in the distance.

The air smells of grass and summer night, and Arizona can hear the crickets, as early into the night as it might be.

"What if the kite isn't flying?" asks Romy mindlessly, fixing her pixie cut in her distorted reflection in the side of the car.

Crosley tugs a sweatshirt from the trunk and over his head, walking towards the path leading to the beach, whacking Romy's head in the process. Folding her towel to her chest, Arizona follows Crosley with Romy in tow. Her bag slaps against her, outline of a thick book imprinting onto Arizona's bare leg in pink lines. The sound of voices steadily gets louder as they near the sand, along with the rush of water to the shore.

Romy accidentally steps on a sharp rock and yells out, gripping Arizona's arm tightly as she limps to the side of the path, where she grabs her foot, staring at it in horror. "Calm the fuck down," mutters Crosley, rolling his eyes, "you're such a gi—" Romy pinches his ear and twists, and he screams a very high-pitched scream.

"You were saying?" she glares, letting her foot sink back into its sandal, and starting towards the beach again.

"Fuck off."

Reaching the edge of the path, where stairs start and sand meets concrete, Arizona flips her flip-flops off, holding the straps around two fingers. The sand is warm and giving under her feet, spreading between her toes. "Man, I love the the beach," says Romy, grinning a giant grin, and smacking her on the head for the second time that day, Crosley makes his way down the stairs, muttering about how Romy is "lame as fuck."

The sky is navy blue, now, and people are silhouettes. Everyone is to the left of the beach, and Arizona spots a pit in which someone is now starting a bonfire. The coals on a barbecue grill burn golden against the dark, and she sees Mrs. Miller, breathing out gladly. Pasting on a bright smile, Arizona bounds up to the woman, who is laughing loudly at something her friend had just said.

"Hey, Laney," Arizona greets the woman, who turns to see the girl, and gathers her up to her chest immediately. Her raven hair is twisted up in a chignon-type thing, and she wears a thin shawl over a pretty, floral sundress. Her deep-set eyes, much identical to not only Jacob's, but also the ocean, crinkle around the edges when she smiles.

"Arizona! How are you, honey?"

"I'm alright, thanks. How are you?"

"Good, good. Are those marshmallows?"

"Oh, yeah, Jeremy told me not to bring anything, but I was think-ing that it could be useful. Like, if we run out, or something."

"That's so sweet of you, thank you! I think Jeremy's over there with a couple of his friends." Smiling thankfully at Mrs. Miller, Arizona waves and walks towards the direction Laney had motioned at, leav-ing Crosley and Romy behind to introduce themselves to Jeremy's mom.

Jeremy, like Laney had said, sits on a log around the firepit, watching as the guy in the middle—who Arizona can now discern is Jacob—chatting with Isaac and another boy she doesn't recognize. As soon as he sees her, he grins hugely, standing up and dusting off his pants to hug her. "This is Nate, and you know Isaac. Nate, this is Arizona."

"Oh, hey!" Nate says immediately, smiling, as if he has finally matched a face to a name. "I've heard about you."

"Really."

"Oooh, yeah," he winks at Arizona, who blushes more out of reflex than anything. Nate is one of those boys that Arizona would never dream of speaking to at school. His black hair is cut close to his head and his skin is the color of coffee with milk, and his eyes are as green as the entire state. They send a jolt through Arizona, and she looks away. Why in hell are all of Jeremy's friends so pretty, anyway?

Romy and Crosley finally stumble towards them, Romy kicking sand up at Crosley, who yells profanities at her. Grumbling, he trudges to them to sit down on the log next to Arizona's, Romy on Arizona's right. She ends up right nest to Nate, and after greeting Jeremy and Isaac, she turns to him. She doesn't say anything for a moment, before pushing out a hello. As flustered as Romy is, she will not stutter. Romy does not stutter. It's actually not really fair, at all.

Nate's smile is easy and even a little bit flirtatious, and Romy looks over her shoulder to make big eyes at Arizona. Oh, my God? they say, and Arizona nods rapidly, I know! Biting her lip, Romy turns back around to engage the boy in a conversation, something she is insanely good at. In the same moment, heat immediately hitting Arizona's face. She narrows her eyes into a squint, watching as Jacob cries out in success and tosses some pieces of wood into the fire before walking around to where the others sit. "Anybody want drinks?" he asks, and he apparently hasn't seen Arizona yet, and there's this almost deflating feeling in her chest. "Eh, whatever, I'm just going to get a pack of sodas. And no alcohol for you, Jer-Bear."

"Don't call me that, man," Jeremy groans, rolling his eyes.

"I think it's cute," laughs Jacob before shaking his head and walking away to the table food is set up on. Arizona nudges Jeremy lightly, smile small.

"I think it's kind of cute, too."

"You're kind of cute."

"Oh."

A laugh erupts from Arizona's right then, apparently from Nate. Romy can be super charming and funny when she wants to be, which is ridiculous, because no one should be given that much people skill in one body. Nate already looks entranced with the blonde (Romy, not Arizona) and Jeremy sees it too.

"Their kids'd be really pretty," says Arizona conversationally and he knocks her outstretched foot with his.

"That's true."

Arizona lets out a startled laugh, unsuspecting of this answer.

"Do you want kids, Jeremy?"

"Please tell me you're not demanding that I propose to you right now," he says in a tone only half-joking.

"Well, I mean...''

"I swear, I will leave right now if you are," he threatens with a small, cute smile, and Arizona giggles.

"I'm not, don't worry. Just asking, though." Arizona doesn't even know her own answer to this. She's read tons of books, watched thousands of movies in which that one line came up, but has never actually pondered the question. The only time she'd ever heard it spoken aloud in real life had been when Gem had asked the group and Crosley had laughed loudly, and that had been the end of that conversation. And now, as she asks her boyfriend the question and waits for an answer, she finds that she couldn't care less about it. And that really gets her angry with herself.

"Huh. Wow, well I've never really thought about it much, before," says Jeremy, shaking his head. "I mean, I think it'd be pretty cool to be a dad. Y'know, take them camping and teaching them how to ride a bike and stuff. But I also kinda want my kid to be legitimate, you know, and for that I have to be married so," he laughs, as does Arizona, trailing off. "How about you?"

"Same. Except for the dad part, obviously. I don't know. I mean, this is the first relationship I've really been in, so I just feel as if it's weirdly impossible that I'm going to be married some time in the future."

"Yeah, exactly." Arizona has the best conversations with her boyfriend. Very couple-y.

Later into the night, once the sky has blackened out completely and everybody has dinner in their stomachs, Arizona sits by herself on a log near the fire. Jeremy had told her that he is going to go swimming with Isaac, and Nate and Romy were walking alone somewhere, and Crosley had seen someone he knows, and gone to talk to them a few minutes ago. Jeremy had asked if Arizona wanted to come, but the night had cooled down considerably and the last thing Arizona wants is a cold in the middle of the summer.

She wishes she had worn jeans or a skirt instead of the cotton shorts she has on, and she winds her arms around her bare knees. She had begged Crosley for his sweatshirt, and he had finally given it up, forcing her to promise him a free meal at The Number at some point. She stares at the fire for a long time before looking to her right, at the ocean she can't seen anymore, just hear. White spots appear to cloud her vision momentarily. And then, Jacob arrives.

"Arizona May," he says languidly, grin slow and warm like the bonfire. He holds a white paper cup in his right hand, and a towel in his left, which he tousles his hair with. It's obvious that he had been in the water. He'd changed out of his jeans from before into a pair of cargo shorts and a dark sweatshirt.

"Hi, Jacob."

"Didn't know you were coming."

"Well, I'm here," Arizona says and he raises his eyebrows, leaning forward to rest his forearms on his knees. Jacob places the towel next to him on the log and puts the rim of the cup to his lips, shooting her a look before taking a sip. "Were you swimming, or something?"

"I was actually just barely in the water, but then Dipshit Jeremy ran into me and dunked me under. So I had to change," he rolls his eyes and sighs, but with a smile. The fire traces bouncing shadows on his face, which somehow looks more angular. They are silent for a moment, and Arizona places her chin in her cupped hand, looking away from the fire because her eyes get teary when she stares into it for too long.

"Hey Arizona," says Jacob, "did you know that your name means hot oven in Spanish?"

"And it means arid zone in English, I know. And yes, I have asked my parents why they would ever name me that, and their reason is that they thought the name was pretty. Every. Time."

"Well, I would go with the Spanish translation, because I think it fits you very well."

"What?"

"You're hot as an oven."

"Wh—"

"Like, wow, this fire is really freaking hot, I may have outdone myself, yeah? Maybe you should take that sweatshirt off, or something."

Arizona's mouth opens and closes multiple times, and Jacob grins cheekily, fully aware of what she had thought his words meant. Arizona glowers and shoves his arm, making it fall off of his knee and jerk towards the ground suddenly, causing him to start, and grip the cup tighter in his other hand.

"Not cool, Jacob."

"Fuck you."

"Eh."

"Offended."

"Good."

"Please, Arizona May, I know you want to get under this."

"Under what?" she asks, blinking, biting back a smile as she makes a big show out of looking around. "I don't see anything I'd want to get under."

"Mhm." Jacob winks knowingly before covering his mouth with his cup and finishing off the rest of his soda. Arizona so does not want to get under him. Jacob's gross. Ew.

He picks up a wooden stick and a marshmallow from the bag next to him, skewering the white sweet before sticking it in the fire. Jacob twirls it, huge, excited smile in place. He glances down, and his eyebrows rise. "You have big feet," he comments in a passive, flippant manner before smirking and looking back into the fire, where his marshmallow bubbles.

"Excuse me?" Arizona knows that she has big feet, but she's not really used to boys pointing this out to her. She's never really cared about her abnormally large feet, but right now she feels weirdly self—or foot—conscious.

"Feet," he says, looking at her in amusement, "you've got big ones."

"So do you," Arizona retorts before swallowing and realizes that this isn't really the best argument, because having big feet is a good thing for guys. A very good thing.

"You bet I do," he grins cockily and she huffs, looking away. Laughing, he nudges her and mutters, "Kidding." A second later, he looks back at his marshmallow, and yelling, he jerks his hand back, to find his marshmallow on fire. Eyes huge, Jacob waves his hand rapidly, blowing on it anxiously. Rolling her eyes, Arizona leans forward and blows lightly, and finally the fire goes out. Jacob lets out a relieved sigh, and then another defeated one as he stares at his blackened marshmallow with slight sadness. He picks off a piece of the rare white left on the marshmallow and pops it into his mouth.

"Your blows are, like, half-spit," Arizona rolls her eyes again, and Jacob chokes, curling forward over his legs to cough before straightening up again, face red.

"What?" his voice is strangled, half from laughter, and half from the need to keep coughing.

"No—I—I mean, what you were doing to get the fire out! You kept blowing at it but there was a lot of spit, more than air and—oh, my God, stop laughing at me!" Jacob is laughing loud, belly laughter, and he may be crying. After about a bazillion minutes later, he takes a breath and wipes at his eyes, shaking his head.

"Is everything you say this sexual?"

"It's only sexual if you make it sexual," mutters Arizona, shoving two marshmallows into her mouth.

"Well, I made it sexual."

"Goddammit, Jacob."

When it's nearing midnight, the beach has become more ocean waves than talking. There are only a few people left, and the Millers are packing everything up, now, taking the things back to the car. Arizona walks to Mrs. Miller, where she stands putting leftovers in Tupperware.

"Thanks so much for inviting us," says Arizona, "this was really fun."

"Aw, I'm so glad you enjoyed it!" The woman hugs Arizona—again—and pulls back, dusting off the shoulders of Crosley's sweatshirt, which had some sand on it prior to the dusting. "Just follow our car to the beach house, and I'll get your rooms set up."

"Oh." Arizona blinks. "Oh. Oh, no, we were actually just going to go get a room at this inn we passed on the way here," she smiles politely, and Laney flutters her hand. Crosley and Romy appear next to Arizona to listen in on the conversation. Crosley's eyebrows rise in question.

"Hush, you're not going anywhere. It's way too dark to drive, anyway. I'll set up two rooms for you guys. You and Romy can share, and Crosley can have his own, I'm sure Jacob wouldn't mind sleeping on the couch tonight." She smiles at Crosley, who smiles victoriously, no doubt cheering in his mind about getting his own room all to himself fuck yeah!

"It's really f—"

Crosley interrupts Arizona with warning eyes, "You are too kind, really." His smile is charming and it is in these moments that Arizona rolls her eyes the most.

Arizona awakes in the middle of the night, absolutely parched. Jesus, talk about arid zone. Groaning, she sits up slowly, and then flops back down because she is so tired, and so unwillingly to get up. But she's so thirsty. If Cros were here, he'd say something along the lines of, "it took you so long to realize this?"

Sighing in defeat, Arizona swings her legs off the side of the bed and tugs the sweatshirt over her head and slips into her flip flops. Romy turns and looks at the girl in a groggy state of mind. "Zona? What're you doing?"

"Just getting a drink, go back to sleep."

"Thank God." With that, Romy turns back around and yanks her blanket over her head, and a second later her snores resume. Shaking her hair out of her face, Arizona opens the door and steps out, shutting it behind her.

The beach house is wooden and drafty, seemingly relatively old. It smells like the ocean and the first floor is perpetually grainy from the sand that blows in, and apparently Mr. Miller had quit trying to clean it years ago, so everybody just wears shoes around the house. There are chimes and miscellaneous beach things like shells and such out on the front porch, that Arizona can hear in the middle of the night when the window is open.

Arizona clicks on the light in the small kitchen, bathing it in fluorescence. Rubbing a her eyes, she yanks the fridge open and grabs the small carton of milk, pouring out a cup before placing it into the microwave. She tiredly leans against the counter, tapping her fingers against the surface. Arizona glances around the little room, half awake, when she sees someone through the sliding porch door, a shadow, and now she is fully awake.

Sliding the glass door and then the net silently to the side, she leans down to pick up a flip flop lying on the porch. She takes a few steps forward, feet situated so they're ready to run if need be. She just needs to see if she knows the person. A few more steps. She can make out a tall form, messy black hair, t-shirt, pajama pants—oh. Jacob stands looking down at something at his feet.

"Jacob?"

Jerking up in surprise, he whips around to look at Arizona.

"What the fuck."

Arizona bites her lip and walks closer to him.

"What're you doing?"

Glaring at her for a few more seconds, he looks back down at his feet. Except for not, because now she sees something just barely lying in the sand.

"It's a jellyfish. Well, it was. It's dead, now."

"You don't say."

Arizona takes a step forward and Jacob juts his let out, tripping her. Yelping, she slides on the sand, sinking down in a very awkward near-splits.

"What the fuck." She glares and he smirks, peeking at her through his lashes before crouching down to pick up the jellyfish with a stick.

"What are you doing up?"

"I was thirsty, so I came down for some water, but I can't really go back to sleep once I'm up unless I have milk, so I'm microwaving some right now." As if on cue, she can hear the beep of the microwave finishing. "I'm gonna go get that."

Hurrying back to the kitchen, she takes the mug out, and makes her way back to Jacob, except now he's sitting near a sand dune. Feet sinking in the sand, Arizona struggles to climb up to where he sits, and plops down next to him.

Arizona looks at the boy while taking a gulp of the milk, "What about you? Why are you out here?"

"Couldn't sleep. I can almost never sleep when we come here. And the fact that I'm on a couch now doesn' t help either," he adds pointedly, and Arizona smiles sheepishly, curling her hands around the warm mug.

"Sorry about that. But, in my defense, your mom said you wouldn't mind."

"I don't," he laughs, tracing something into the sand with the stick he still has, now rid of the jellyfish. "I can't sleep either way."

"Why can't you sleep?" Arizona leans forward, tucking her hair back behind her ear, shivering slightly from the cold nipping at her legs.

"I have no idea, actually. I think it's because I feel as if the tide's going to come really fast and, like, flood the house of something." He laughs, shaking his head. "It's stupid."

"No, it makes sense, I guess."

They are silent again, Arizona sipping at her milk incredibly loud to her ears. Despite this, she can hear the waves rolling out onto shore, and then back again. They are loud, and unable to be seen. In fact, the only thing she can see right now is her feet directly in front of her. They are really freaking big.

"Hey, can I ask you something?" asks Jacob, and Arizona nods, shrugging. "Why are you still with my brother?"

"What?" Arizona blinks.

"Like, I know it's not my place to ask, and it's nosy and shit, and I respect you not wanting to answer, but if you are willing to answer, why are you still dating Jeremy? I mean, you told me that you don't really like him like that, and honestly? He doesn't seem so obsessed with you, either, and you guys seem more like friends than a couple, and I'm just a bit confused, I guess."

"Man." Arizona sighs, leaning back on her elbows, pressing her mug into the sand next to her to make it stay. "Thanks for bringing that up." Jacob knocks his foot into hers in a way that says "any time." "Want to know the truth?"

"Uh, yeah, I think that's why I asked you."

"Don't need your sass, Jacob. Don't need your sass."

"Sorry. Keep going."

"I..." she trails off, looking into the black hanging low on them. "I have no idea, actually. He's my first boyfriend, you know. And that's pretty exciting, the fact that I have someone to call my boyfriend."

Arizona realizes that she actually does not have any clue as to why she's still dating Jeremy. But now that she is, she can't imagine not dating him. The prospect of breaking up with him is terrifying, and it makes her nervous just thinking about it. Jacob gives her a side-long glance before looking away with his lip tilted up slightly, in that way that makes him look always amused.

"Just a dating tip, Arizona May—and yes, I know, I'm not the ideal person to be giving dating advice, but trust me on this—maybe you should date somebody you actually like. That's what most people do."

16

— • —

Chapter 16

It's a sweltering July afternoon when Jeremy calls Arizona to cover his shift at The Number. Despite the fact that all she wants to do is spend a lazy birthday at Briana's, Arizona can't not help her boyfriend out. He's covered her countless times by now, and who knows, she might make a lot of tips. The place tends to get more business on either really hot or really cold days.

Grunting, Arizona rolls over onto her stomach on the bed for a few seconds before slipping into some flip-flops. Pulling her hair into a ponytail, she grabs her bag before yelling at her mom that she's going out to work. The walk there is only a few minutes, but it feels like years under the sun pounding on her back. Arizona really wishes her permit would become a license overnight. Crosley had agreed to teach her how to drive months ago, but then they had both forgotten about it after the first two (disastrous) times.

Arizona walks into the restaurant-café and can immediately feel her sweat evaporating at the cool air rushing at her face. She had been right, the place is packed with mostly teens. A group of girls huddles over a huge ice-cream, talking amongst one another whilst eyeing a pack of oblivious boys. They are actually pretty hot, and

Arizona makes sure to look straight ahead as she walks past them. There are already too many male figures in her life, as it is.

Brushing a few stray strands of blonde hair from her face, Arizona ties an apron from the back wall around her waist before logging in. She catches Jane's coal-lined eye from across the glass covering the ice-cream, and almost immediately a look of pure relief brushes across the latter's face. Handing a cone to the last person, Jane walks towards where Arizona stands by the register.

"Do you want to take the ice-cream serving job?" she mumbles, but she looks so hopeful that Arizona can't really say no—and that is the second time today.

"Sure," she smiles softly, nudging Jane gently ahead of her to the counter before grabbing the scoop. This morning, when she had woken up, Arizona had been ready to stay at home with a boxed set of Friends and some ice-cream cake, and maybe she had also been ready to flop onto Briana's couch for the rest of the day until Jeremy would take her out to a movie.

A deluge of kids in polka-dotted party hats almost knocks the front door in after half an hour, two women trying their hardest to herd the children to where Arizona stands, grinning subconsciously. Don't get her wrong, Arizona doesn't enjoy taking care of kids for more than an hour, or what goes along with it, but the interactions are always fun, and kids always have something stupid and/or funny to say. It's brilliant.

Tucking a chunk of hair behind her ear, Arizona leans over the glass covering to peer down at the what looks to be kindergartners. "What can I get you guys?" she asks with raised eyebrows, and who is probably the birthday boy jumps excitedly, much to the angst of the unimpressed-looking girl next to her. The boy grins a huge grin missing one of its two front teeth. After multiple tries, he stutters out that he'd like a triple-scoop waffle cone of bubblegum ice-cream—which his mother than lowered to one scoop. ("Mom!" "You can't finish that, Will!" "But, Mommmm!")

Getting everybody a cone takes effort, along with ten minutes (not including the time it takes for everybody to order). An hour later, there are even more people crowding The Number, and Arizona is so very glad to be getting out. Grabbing a tray to pile dirty dishes on, she pushes the kitchen door open to put them in the sink. Jacob's already there, sliding food onto a plate. He glances over his shoulder to see her, and that same, easy smile slides onto his lips.

"Hey."

"Hi," Arizona smiles a little, putting the tray on the counter and grabbing a mug to rinse out and put in the dishwasher.

"Jeez, you'd think no one would want hamburgers in this weather. Fuckin' weird, man."

Arizona hums in agreement, squeezing soap into a glass and following it with a sponge. They are both quiet for a few minutes, the only sound the squishing of soap and water, and the quiet CD player on a shelf.

"So," says Jacob, finally breaking the silent waves, "do you know what school you're going to?"

"Yeah, actually. NYU."

"Hey, no way!" His head flips up in a jerky motion and he looks over at her with a huge, blinding, ridiculously fucking perfect grin.

"Yeah, why?"

"I'm going there, too."

"Wait. Seriously?"

"Yeah."

The conversation settles again, and Arizona watches as an interesting expression twists at Jacob's features.

"Oh, my God," he mutters, pausing what he had been doing and wiping his hands down his apron before running one through his hair, mussing it up. "I'm going to be seeing you more than Jeremy." He doesn't say it with as much panic as his gestures suggest he will, but Arizona kind of makes up for that in the inside, because she's freaking out. It's already bad as it is that she sees this much of her boyfriend's older brother, and somehow it just got worse, because she'll be going to the same school as him for at least the next four years.

It's awkwardly quiet for a few seconds before Arizona blurts out, "You're doing architecture, right?"

"I don't know, I'll probably change it. Maybe nurse? My mom'll like that. How about you?"

"I was thinking that I could maybe be a therapist," mumbles Arizona, putting the last plate in the dishwasher. Jacob snorts, smiling. "What?"

"From what I've seen, you talk more about yourself with the patient, than about them."

"Oh, hush, you don't know me, you don't know my life."

"Actually..."

"I don't fucking need your sass, Jacob."

Drying her hands on a rag, Arizona hangs her apron on the hook by the door and leaves, hollering a goodbye to Jacob and Jane over her shoulder. It's fucking hot, outside. Arizona needs a freaking license. Maybe she should ask Crosley to teach her, again.

Cutting across Washington High's field, Arizona avoids the soccer team and heads towards Briana's house, where she can hopefully laze the rest of the day away. Her family had stopped making such a big deal out of birthdays when each of the girls turned twelve, and now, they usually just mean that she can do whatever she wants the entire day, as long as she's back home by midnight. It's really actually quite great.

Arizona knocks on Briana's door twice, the one that Briana's dad had made the mistake of painting red a couple years ago. A second later there are footsteps audible from the other side, and then the sound of locks turning the other way, and the door finally swings open. It's Briana's younger brother. He's currently sixteen, a junior in high school, and doesn't give a shit about anything that is not good music and skateboards. His eyes are always red, him seemingly always tired, and Arizona is not sure whether it actually is due to lack of sleep or maybe something much more questionable. He used to really scare Arizona despite him being younger than her, but he's actually very nice once you get to know him.

"Hey, Raymond," Arizona smiles and he nods, eyes hooded before stepping back and walking back towards the kitchen, leaving the door open for Arizona to step through.

"Hey. Briana's probably in her room."

"Thanks."

As Raymond says, Briana's on her back, spread out over her blue bedspread. Several DVDs scatter around her, laptop open and playing music at her desk. Arizona kicks the door and Briana shoots up with a start.

"Happy birthday!"

"Thanks, Briana," Arizona grins, returning the hug Briana had bustled up from the bed to give.

"So, I picked out all of your favorite comedies slash rom-coms because you're a lame-o who doesn't like watching action films or horrors on her birthday, which, by the way, is very weird. I had to put all of them on hold at the library since last month to get them by now. The things I do for you," Briana sighs dramatically, flopping back onto her bed, followed by Arizona soon after. "How about 10 Things I Hate About You? Oooh, The Wedding Singer? You've Got Mail?"

"Maybe Stuck In Love?"

"Magic Mike?"

"Briana, you have a girlfriend."

"I know, I just thought you might want to. Penises scare me, anyway," she whispers the last part and Arizona laughs, shaking her head as she slides the disc for 500 Days of Summer into the player.

At five forty-five, once the two girls have gone through two movies and Briana's closet once, Arizona's phone rings and she twists around to grab it, back cracking in the process. "Ew," mumbles Briana around some popcorn.

"Hello?" Arizona rests back onto the bed, and Briana attempts balancing the near empty bowl of candy on her left knee. Briana had forced her into a blue dress of her own, because she believes that one must always look fucking brilliant for dates on one's birthday. Arizona actually hadn't put up much of a fight either, because the dress is actually quite cute, with a soft skirt that brushes the tops of her knees and sleeves that reach her elbows.

"Arizona May."

"What do you want, Jacob."

"Jeremy gave me your number."

"Why."

"I need you to cover my six o'clock shift."

"What? But Jeremy was taking me to a movie!"

"Huh. Well, he never had a problem with giving me your number to ask for a cover. Cancel it. I've covered you so many times, man."

"Ugh."

Ok so maybe Jeremy and Jacob have covered Arizona countless times. It's whatever.

"Please, Arizona May? Anyway, you owe me for both those times I've pretended to be your boyfriend, so far."

Well, the boy had her there. Groaning, she rubs a hand down her face,

"Fine." She think of telling him it's her birthday, maybe it'll lead to some softening of the heart, but before she can mention it, she hears him hang up with a click, and then the dial tone. For the second time that day, Arizona slides off a bed with an angry sigh. The bowl falls to the carpeted floor and Briana curses.

"Who was that?" she asks mindlessly, leaning over to pick the bowl back up and put it on the desk. She looks back at Arizona with raised eyebrows, who frowns.

"Jacob. He wants me to cover him."

"When?"

"Now. Can I borrow your bike?"

"I'll drive you, c'mon, Birthday Girl."

The drive in Romy's mom's minivan is quick, but when the two arrive at the restaurant-café, it looks nearly empty. "That's weird," mutters Arizona, and with furrowed eyebrows, Briana follows Arizona. ("I'm not letting your death be because of some killer clown in an empty restaurant-café, Zona.")

The door is open, weirdly enough, when Arizona opens it, and though the lights are off, there is still light filtering in through the many windows. The entire room is empty, and Arizona is not sure whether the store is open or not. Just as she turns to check the sign again, someone jumps out from behind the counter, yelling her a happy birthday.

Arizona screeches in terror and then the light is on and her friends are jumping out from behind tables, and Crosley is knocking a chair over and jamming his toe into a table leg in the midst of wishing her a happy birthday, which then comes out more of a "Happ - sonuvafuckingbitchmotherofGodthatfuckinghurtsJesus-fuckingChristowowowow."

Briana is grinning from beside the blonde, whose chest is heaving like crazy.

"You knew about this?" Arizona demands, and Briana shrugs. "How did you hide this so well, Crosley is shit at keeping secrets."

"And that's why you haven't interacted with him this week." Briana laughs, hugging her. The rest of the friends trail over to where they stand, mostly just to laugh at Arizona and make fun of her surprised face. Jeremy's there too, smile wide and killer.

"You knew about this?" Arizona asks him and he shrugs, scratching the back of his neck.

"Jeremy actually helped with a lot of the planning," says Gem, and Arizona's eyebrows rise. She really wishes he hadn't, but he's really freaking adorable for doing this, so she hugs him tightly before thanking him.

"I'm still taking you to the movie," he tells her, and Arizona's smile somehow grows.

"Sounds like a plan."

Later, after the really delicious cake that Arizona had somehow eaten, even after all the popcorn and candy, she goes to the kitchen to put her dish in the sink, and there's Jacob, washing some things up. She had only seen him a few times outside, and he had mouthed a happy birthday to her before retreating back to the kitchen. She hasn't gotten to speak to him yet tonight, seeing as the rare times he was outside was just to talk to Jeremy.

"Hey, Jacob," says Arizona, eyebrows raised.

"Arizona May," he nods at her over his shoulder.

"What are you doing here?"

"I was actually going to be here to clean the place, but then Jeremy told me about your birthday party, and he asked if I would make the cake, so. No one's paying me, though. It's a favor, I guess."

"So now I owe you for another thing?"

"You said it, not me."

A second passes, and then Arizona hears what Jacob had just said a second ago.

"You baked that cake?" Arizona asks, mouth gaping, eyes huge.

"Mhm."

"That's a really freaking good cake, Jacob."

"Why, thank you." He grins, wiping his hands on a dishtowel before turning around to face her finally. "You look quite ravishing tonight," Jacob smiles a surprisingly genuine smile that holds less humor than usual, and her heart stops.

Arizona freezes, unsure whether to run away or to laugh, but as it seems, she doesn't quite get to make that decision for herself because now she is choking.

"What did you just say?" she barely gets out and he grins an incredibly cheesy grin.

"You know exactly what I said."

Shaking her head, she looks up at him, and without meaning too she becomes stuck and she can't move and apparently her eyes can't look away because they're not and fuckshitgoddammit.

"Stop that!"

"What?" he asks, laughing lightly.

"That!" she exclaims, creating a circle in the air with her index finger near his eyes. "That thing you do with your eyes! Stop it!"

"I don't know what you mean!" He's laughing actual shoulder-shaking laughs now. It may be the best sound Arizona has ever heard in her life.

"You know exactly what I mean! You know what you're doing! Stop that!"

"Why should I stop when it's working?"

Arizona widens her eyes. "You do know that you're doing it, you fucking douchecanoe!"

"What did you just call me?" he laughs even harder, and Jacob is almost crying now, a thin film of glossiness over his eyes. Adorably boyish creases are forming at the corners of his laughing eyes and shit, Arizona is in deep.

"I called you a douchecanoe!"

"I think you just call everybody you're in love with a douchecanoe," Jacob says with a smirk, leaning forward slightly.

"What—no, I'm not!"

"Yep, you are." Though his voice is nothing more than teasing, Arizona is getting panicked, trying to tell him that she is absolutely, certainly, most definitely not in love with him.

"Nu-uh."

"Yu-huh. See, you're blushing! It is working!"

"It is not working!"

"Yes it is," he smirks slowly, smugly, walking closer to her and she is walking back.

"Stoppit!" she squeals, melding all her words together into one big sticky mess.

"Wanna know how I know it's working?"

"No, because it's...not—," her swallow is loud, "—because it's not working!"

He opens his mouth again, ready to throw another line back at her for her to fumble with, but by then she is against the kitchen door and if she leans forward his lips will brush her forehead and she has to physically restrain her hands by wrapping them into fists and pressing them into the door on either side of her body, just so they don't reach up and brush the hair falling into his ocean eyes out of his face.

"Stop that," she says in a voice that sounds just as faint as she feels. "It's not...it's notworking." Again her words mesh together but this time it is only because she has to fit them into the receding space between their mouths as she presses them together. There is a second of hesitation in which Arizona is terrified that the decision she has made is even worse than it should be because he isn't responding, but then he is kissing her back just as hard and just as fast and his hand is at the back of her neck, pressing their lips even closer to each other until they are just like Arizona's words, and his other is at her waist, pushing her into the door. She is on her tiptoes and he aligns himself with her. Arizona moans, she moans, and he pulls back slightly, so that when he laughs she feels it on her lips.

"What was that?" he breathes. "Was that a moan? Was that it working?"

"Shut the fuck up." She is about to tilt her head to his again, but he beats her to him and God, Arizona should be worrying about the fact that she is kissing Jeremy's older (much hotter) brother in Jeremy's family's restaurant's kitchen, especially seeing as he is right outside, but all she can even begin to think about is how fucking glad she is that they are against the door and that Jacob has just locked it.

"This is so bad, I'm so fucking fucked," she mumbles as he presses chaste kisses down her jaw, and she feels it when his lips form their smile.

"Happy birthday, by the way. You're legal."

Arizona barely hears what he's said, and she's way too intoxicated to even process what his insinuating. She groans, partly from Jacob's lips on her skin and partly from how wrong all this is, and then she is gently pushing him off her, stumbling away. It's as if she is electricity and once she goes out, so does he, and suddenly his eyes are widening in that panic that was inevitable and he's walking back, away from her, to the other side of the kitchen, having to lean back against the counter.

"Wha—holy shit. Fuck. Shit. Son of a fucking bitch, oh, my God."

Arizona's fingers that had been covering her lips fall to her side, and her hair into her face.

"Jeremy hasn't even kissed you yet, has he."

It's a statement more than a question, yet Arizona still shakes her head, swallowing hard. Jacob curses again, swollen lips pursed. Arizona hates herself for wanting to kiss him again.

"Maybe, um," Arizona coughs and looks anywhere but him. "Maybe we shouldn't spend so much time together. Maybe that's the problem."

"Yeah," Jacob nods rapidly, "yeah, let's do that. It'll be really productive, too, seeing as we're even going to the same school next year!" he says with mock excitement.

"Okay, stop with the sass, you ass."

"Did you know it? That you're a poet?"

"Stop." Arizona laughs, biting her kissed lips hard.

"Why?" he asks, and the humor is in his expression again, but he is still looking conflicted.

"Because I might kiss you again."

"Yeah, I guess I should stop, then," he chokes out, running a hand through his hair angrily. Taking a second to catch her breath, Arizona swallows and fixes her hair, her dress.

"I'm going to go. Thanks for all of this," she says, small smile fixed. He nods, and she turns to yank open the kitchen door. As she opens it, somebody else pushes it in, and she stumbles back to avoid being hit by the door. It's Jeremy, and his face is happy and smiling and oblivious, and another wave of shame hits Arizona, nearly pulling her under. Why is she so stupid? Why?

"You want to go for that movie?" he asks, and forcing herself to not look at Jacob, Arizona nods and grins. Jeremy smiles and walks back to the front door, and as she shuts the door, Arizona looks back to see Jacob rubbing his hair in rough, jerky, angry motions. He doesn't look at her, and Arizona closes the door. As Arizona walks out of The Number to Jeremy's car, she realizes something. And it kills Arizona a little bit to realize this, but she can't help but think that so far, this has been her best birthday yet. And it's not just because of the surprise party.

17

CHAPTER 17

Suffice to say, Arizona May is screwed.

She and the four others are currently splayed across a green lawn downtown. The Saturday Market is a once-a-week thing in this part of the city, where everybody who wants to-mostly hippies and over-priced jewelry sellers-sets up stalls, and it's the most people Arizona ever sees in one spot at the same time.

They sit with tacos and Italian sodas away from the crowd in a field, some families and other people picnicking some distance away. Arizona had just told everybody what exactly went down a week and a day ago. It had taken her long enough, but now she has, it still hasn't relieved much of anything from her. "Damn," says Romy, pushing her glasses up to rest on her forehead, and leans back on her elbows, legs stretched out before her, towards Gem.

"Jhyeah," snorts Crosley, shaking his head, "Arizona May, more like Arizona Mess."

Gem smacks his arm and he kicks her soda over, spilling all of the orange contents out onto the grass.

"The hell," whines Gem, scowling. "Go buy me another one. Now. Dick."

"You're such a bossy scrub."

"You're a child, go buy me one right now, Crosley." Gem glares at him hard, and he watches her expressionlessly for a few long moments before sighing and getting up. On his way towards he food stands, he throws his jacket over her head, and Arizona can hear Gem's huff.

"Anyway," says Briana, smirking at Gem's flushed face. She turns to Arizona again, scratching her straight, black hair. "Zona, you do know that you're going to have to break up with Jeremy, right?"

"What?" says Arizona, blankly. She knew that they would say that, but she didn't think that they would come right out and say it. She thought that maybe they would brainstorm ideas with her or something, at least humor her for a little while.

"I mean, you're going to college. You're both going to college. Long distance relationships never work, man," Briana shrugs, picking at the ends of her hair, studying them for split ends. And Arizona realizes that Briana is right, and she had been so stupid that she hadn't even thought about that, yet. College isn't even that far away, either-move-in day is at the end of the month. She'd already started packing up some of her things in brown boxes. Arizona has no clue what the hell is going to happen with her relationship.

"Relationship."

"You gotta break up with him," says Romy, pushing her sunglasses back over her eyes, again. "You don't even like him, it'll be alright."

"But he's so sweet-"

"-and cute, and funny, and nice, and you could never do that, ever, yeah, we know, Arizona." Crosley shows up suddenly, throwing another glass bottle of orange soda at Gem, who catches it impressively. "It's going to happen one way or another. Save some dignity, break up with him."

"But-"

"Just," Romy fixes her with a hard look, "do it. It'll be better for everyone."

Arizona sighs in compliance. "Bossy scrub," Crosley coughs into his curled fist.

Arizona is going to do it, too. She makes up her mind to break up with Jeremy right after her shift at The Number. She also braces herself to accept not working there anymore, after this. Not like she wants to with her ex-boyfriend-soon to be ex-boyfriend.

And now, as she hangs up her apron, she hiccups. Freaking nerves. She's never done this before. It's pretty terrifying, she must say. She has some new-found respect for those players that do this seven times a week. (Not really.)

Another hiccup wrecking her body, Arizona slowly walks to the counter and slides into a stool. Jeremy is wiping the surface of the counter, and his smile is instant when he sees her. "Hey, what're you still doing here?"

"I-hic-just wanted to talk with you, that's all."

"Oh, okay. Do you want a glass of water?"

"Y-hic-eah, please."

Laughing, he slides a glass of ice-water over to her side of the counter.

"So..." he trails off into a pulsed second, picking at a chip in the counter. "Oh, there's this new sci-fi movies out, I thought you mi-"

"Jeremy, I-hic-I, uh, I think-hic-I think we should break up."

Arizona stumbles on all her words and even squeezes in too hiccups here and there, but Jeremy's heard her, and he blinks at her once, two times. And then, much to her bewilderment, another burst of laughter wisps from his mouth, and then it's Arizona's turn to blink.

"Oh, thank God."

"What?"

"I was going to say the same thing. Not in that moment, but at some point."

"Oh, man, really?"

Arizona's hiccups are gone.

"Yeah," he grins and then Arizona's laughing, too, and she can't stop, she is so relieved. If this is what breaking up with someone feels like, then what's the whole deal with it? After a few more moments of unhinged, a little bit crazed laughter, Arizona coughs and takes a sip of her water. Jeremy looks around the restaurant to see the few people there already served, and he hangs his apron up, coming around to sit next to her.

"Can I ask you something?" she asks.

"'Course."

"Did you actually like me, like, romantically the entire time we were going out?"

Biting his lip, jeremy traces something in the condensation on his glass.

"...No."

Arizona's eyebrows disappear behind her hair.

"Oh."

"I liked you for the first few months. But, I don't know, at some point my feelings for you just...become platonic."

"Why didn't you break up with me, then?" Arizona smiles, finding this all too amusing.

"I actually really liked hanging out with you, though, so I was scared that if we did, we wouldn't talk, anymore," he admits, and Arizona's eyes crinkle.

"That's stupid, of course we would. We will," she adds. Jeremy grins his killer grin and nods once, a resolute nod. "I'm still allowed to work here, then, right?" Arizona asks, tone only slightly worried, and Jeremy's smile softens.

"Of course."

"Awesome. So it's a mutual uncoupling, then. Nobody broke up with anybody," says Arizona.

"Mutual uncoupling," confirms Jeremy.

Arizona slides off the stool and grabs her bag before pausing and turning back. Jeremy is headed back towards the kitchen, and Arizona can feel hiccups rising again.

"Wait, Jeremy."

The boy turns towards her, eyebrows risen questioningly.

"There's something else."

"Yeah?"

"I...I kissed Jacob."

"And he was totally fine with it?" Crosley snorts, shaking his head and taking a right. A car cuts in front of him and he rests his arm on the horn, making it blare loudly until Arizona whacks his arm. Crosley is angriest when on the road. It's funny when the anger isn't directed at her.

"Yeah, man, it was really weird. Like, his new girlfriend-one that actually likes him-is going to be really lucky."

"Are you sure he's not gay?"

"Pretty sure. All he said at first was that he'd kind of done the same thing to Jacob, before-but, not exactly the same, because rumor has it, Jacob and Jan were on a break. She was sad or something, and she kissed her, and he eventually kissed her back because, and I quote, "when a sad girl kisses you, you can't just reject them." I told him that many people do that, and sometimes kissing drunk girls back is called taking advantage of them, and he asked me whose side I'm on."

"I dunno, maybe he wants to stay friends with you just so he can see more of me. I've seen him looking at me a few times." Crosley flexes his muscle jokingly, and Arizona snorts.

"Yeah, because you're such a conceited, annoying prick."

Crosley parks at the shoulder of the road, leaning over to open Arizona's door.

"Get out," he says.

"Drive," Arizona rolls her eyes.

"Ge-"

"Drive."

"Only because I want to," mutters Crosley, getting back onto the road. "Only because I want to."

Two songs later, they pull into the rehabilitation center parking lot. Arizona's here to say goodbye to everybody before she has to take that exciting yet scary plane to New York. Arizona moves to get out of the car, but then a realization hits her and she sits back in her seat. Her grin is so huge that Crosley becomes wary.

"What."

"You know what this means, right?"

"What what means, Arizona, just tell me, dammit," he grumbles, looking through his CDs.

"I broke up with Jeremy. That means you have to ask Gem out."

The CD case falls out off his hand and Crosley curses.

"But now wouldn't even be the best time, because college and-"

"And you can figure it out for yourselves. But keep up your end of the deal, buddy."

"Don't call me that, I'm not a dog."

"Actually-"

"Leave."

Laughing, Arizona does.

By now, some of the rehabees have left the center, for various reasons. Arizona enters the activities center and Adeeb and James sit on the couch, knitting needles in both of their hands.

"No," she hears Adeeb sigh exasperatedly, "loop it, dammit, James."

"I'm sorry."

"Aren't you artsy, or whatever? Aren't you supposed to be good with your hands?"

"That's what she said," Amberley, another girl sitting on the ground beneath them, snorts. Adeeb leans over to look at her, face unbelieving.

"You're four, I swear to God."

James sees her first, waving slightly.

"Arizona May!" says Adeeb, and Arizona hears Jacob. Jesus, she needs to get a hold of herself. She can't have feelings for her ex-boyfriend's older brother, that is so socially unacceptable. "James has something for you." Arizona smiles and her eyes flit to the blonde boy, who itches his neck.

"Yeah, like for college and stuff."

"Oh, wow, that is so nice!" Arizona grins. She's known these people for more than a year, and it's so weird to think that she won't see them every month, anymore.

"Here," says James, holding up a rolled-up piece of sketch paper. Arizona unfurls it, and there's her, smiling down at something on the ground. It may or may not be Adeeb's shoe that Evan-who, she finds, is now gone, as well-had thrown. She can see every tiny stroke of the pencil, and she really wishes she could draw, too. It's incredible.

"Holy crap, James, this is amazing! Thank you." Arizona is pretty sure she's not supposed to touch them, but she hugs him, anyway, and when she pulls back, James is flustered, scratching his neck, again. Adeeb smirks.

"So," says Lisa, who's just come strolling up to them. "What's going on with that hot guy you're always complaining about?"

"Okay, I am not."

Amberly snorts and Arizona rolls her eyes.

"I'm supposed to be asking you guys how you're doing," Arizona complains, and Adeeb waves it away, sitting down across from her and resting his chin on his palm.

"Your problems are very interesting, Arizona. Amuse us."

"Oh, wow."

18

—— ◦ ——

CHAPTER 18

B en ends up coming to New York with her. She likes to think that she is relatively independent, but doesn't even try to deny the fact that she is so grateful to have her dad there, because God knows that she wouldn't even be able to catch a taxi from the airport.

It's an incredibly hot day, when she moves in. Getting all her boxes and suitcases into the hall is difficult enough, and the other students with their families aren't really helping either. It's quite the process moving everything into her dorm, which she finds empty when she arrives.

Grunting, Ben tosses the last box down on her bed, sitting down after it. "Thanks, Dad," smiles Arizona, falling into the desk chair. He only grunts again, in response. The room is small, room for only two naked beds, two wooden desks, and two dressers. In the back, doors open to reveal two closets.

"Better than I had," says Ben, and laughing, Arizona leans down to get her bedspread out of a brown box labeled Bed (and probably other stuff). "Well," he gets up, smacking the bed post. "I'll be in that hotel near the campus, just call if you need anything. I'm leaving tomorrow night. Let's have lunch, yeah?"

"Sure. Thanks." Arizona gives him a hug before he leaves. "Bye, Dad."

"Bye, Arizona."

The door creaks shut, and then Arizona is alone, once again. She sighs and unzips her suitcase, starting to hang up the clothes.

Everyone except for Gem, who had left for college last week, is still back home. Romy is staying in-state to go to the community college, Briana is going to Vermont in a day, and Crosley is driving down to California on the twenty-fifth, because he had gotten into Berkeley. It isn't Columbia—which Arizona is a little bumbed about, because if it had been, then they'd be able to visit each other—but Crosley had still been incredibly excited.

The door opens again, behind Arizona, and when she turns, there's a girl in the threshold, tapping something on her phone with furrowed eyebrows, before looking up to meet Arizona's eyes. An instant smile spreads on her red lips, and she walks forward with an outstretched hand.

"You must be Arizona."

"And you're Priya?" Arizona shakes her ring-covered hand.

"Yes, I am," she grins, running a hand through her straight, black hair.

From what Arizona had found, looking through her roommate's Facebook profile, Priya is a sophomore, she is single, and she doesn't go to many parties, which is very important to Arizona, because she'd rather be sleeping, than—anything else, really.

"I was thinking we could loft the beds and put the desks under," says Priya, looking around their room, "it'll give us more space."

"Definitely."

The rest of the morning is spent fixing up the room, and Priya offers to take Arizona around campus, to the plaza, where the Club Rush is. She keeps the door unlocked behind her as she follows Arizona down the hall. When Arizona stops abruptly, Priya makes a noise of surprise, stumbling back. Because Arizona didn't think that her luck could get any worse, but apparently it could, since Jacob is right in front of them, turning the handle of a door to his left, box resting in his other arm.

Are you kidding me?

Jacob doesn't see them, and he disappears inside the room, and Arizona stealthily slides against the wall, trying to sneak past the gaping door, but alas, she has never been the sneaky type, as she finds out in the next second.

"Ariz—what the hell?"

"What?" Arizona blinks about a thousand times, pasting on a bewildered smile. "Jacob? What are you doing here?" Sure she had known that he'd be attending the same school as her, but not that he'd be living in the same building as her! This is insane.

"I'm helping Derek move in." The pressure is gone from her chest just as fast, and Arizona smiles. Another boy in a hat from inside peeks around the corner and nods at Arizona. Derek, probably.

"Oh," she says, but she is saying ohthankGod on the inside. She can feel Priya's confused gaze on the back of her head.

"Do you live here?"

"'Yep."

"Cool, cool."

"Yep."

"I'll see you later, then, I guess."

"Yep."

"Bye, Arizona."

May. Arizona May.

"Yep."

She can only breathe once she's out of the building and outside, again, sun bright on her face. Priya breathes a laugh from next to her, raising an arm to block the sun from her eyes. "What was that?"

"Jacob."

"He's hot."

"God, I know."

"What happened there?" asks Priya conversationally, bounding down the cement steps to the sidewalk. Arizona only follows her, no idea where the path is taking her.

"I dated his younger brother. And we kissed. His brother and I are broken up, now—well, mutual uncoupling." Priya hisses a breath through her teeth.

"Did you guys kiss before or after you broke up?"

Arizona doesn't think about how she is basically telling her life story to this girl she had just met (life story of the past year, but life story, nonetheless).

"Before."

"Oh, shit."

"Yeah, but Jeremy, his brother, was totally fine with it. Which is really freaking weird, but I'm not complaining," laughs Arizona.

"You keep good company."

"I like to think so," Arizona hums in agreement.

They are on a busy street, now, people sliding past them on either side, and Priya pays this no mind, while Arizona is totally uncomfortable. It's so different from back home, with little stalls set up along the streets, shops on the other side. The pavement is burning underfoot. Priya tugs Arizona into a small corner shop, where it smells like pizza and summer. Arizona follows the other girl to the back corner, where three other girls sit, a boy cutting in front of them to the exit. Arizona doesn't miss the small smile Priya sends his way. She makes a note to self to ask about the green-eyed beauty later.

"This is Arizona, my roommate," says Priya, grin wide. Arizona waves a small wave, smile a bit awkward. The three girls chorus their hello, and Priya proceeds to introduce them. Tara is a tall, pretty red-head, who is best friends with Ha-Young, a transfer student from Japan with black eyes and porcelain skin. Heather is short and nice, with unruly, black curls and caramel eyes, and she is the only freshman.

Tara and Ha-Young leave an hour later, talking about how they're getting a new roommate at their loft today. The other three girls are left to finish the veggie pizza on their own. Later, Priya and Heather take Arizona to the plaza, where the promised Club Rush is.

Arizona lets them sign her up for whatever, deciding that she'll pick and choose later. Except for sports. She makes is very clear to them beforehand, that she does not do sports. When they get back to their room—Heather comes with—Jacob is long gone, and Arizona wishes that the same thing would happen w ith her crush on him.

"I ran into Jacob, today."

"Already?"

Arizona can hear Gem's risen eyebrows through the phone.

"Yep. I almost threw up. I was so scared that he would be living in the same dorm as me, but apparently he was just helping his friend move in."

"Was this friend hot?"

"He was alright, why?"

"I dunno, maybe you could get with him and make Jacob jealous."

"Okay, uh, I've already gotten with his brother, I think I'm good."

"And it worked, didn't it? He kissed you."

"I kissed him, actually."

A series of crinkles proceed, and Gem informs Arizona that she is applauding her.

"Hey, you know who is cute, though?"

"Oooh, who?"

"Well, I mean, I think he's gross, but you find him cute, so."

"No—"

"Cr—"

"Don't d—."

"Crosss—"

"Don't say it. Don't fucking say i—."

"Crosley."

"Goddammit, Arizona."

19

— ● —

CHAPTER 19

Arizona is ten minutes early to Psychology. It's her first day and she would very much rather be early than late. She has two today, and this first one starts at eight in the morning, though her first one tomorrow begins at noon. She'd been forced to get up early, and she'd thankfully had enough time to get a coffee on the way, from a cute, cheap place called Teacup that Ha-Young had told her about.

It's a cold morning, and the wisps of smoke curling off the top of the paper cup clasped between her hands blow away as quickly as they rise. Sniffling, Arizona pulls the door to the building open, and finds a hall smaller than she had expected, with eleven rows of folded seats curling around the room. There are already a few people strewn about the chairs, the few that know each other conversing in low tones, some freshmen uncertainly organizing their materials once and then again, the odd one sleeping in a corner. Arizona sits down in a seat near the center of the chairs, setting her bag down by her legs and pushing her glasses back up her nose. They help her see, help her look smart, and help her feel smart.

A girl with crazy, black curls sits down and Arizona bites her lip before opening her mouth. "Heather?" She's unsure whether it's really her, or not, but when the girl turns around, Arizona lets out a small breath and smiles. "It is you."

"Hey! Hold on, let me move." She proceeds to grab all her things in her arms, just barely carrying them the short distance to the seat next to Arizona. Heather plops down in the chair with a grin. "I was so scared I'd be alone. Why are you taking Psych?"

"Therapist."

"Oooh, that sounds fun. I don't know what I'm doing, yet. Probably doctor, or a nurse. I mean, I want to write, but my mom would kill me if I majored in anything not even slightly related to math or science." Arizona laughs, nodding in agreement. It's scary how relevant that sentence is to her life.

Suddenly, a cup slams down on the desk next to her. No one but Jacob sits down next to her, and he sits down as if there's a thousand pounds weighing down on him. She can hear music blaring through the headphones covering his ears, and he looks tired, with violet skin under his eyes that might have been there before, but had gone unnoticed, if so. He rubs at his eyes and reclines back in the chair, looking like he is trying very hard to keep his eyes open. Arizona raises her eyebrows, first because Jacob is in her first freaking class—and she is so not happy with her luck, right now—and second because he looks like death.

"You look like death," says Arizona, if a bit hesitantly. She's not sure whether it's okay to talk to him, yet, especially since the last time she'd seen him, he'd called her Arizona without the May. But, seeing as he'd taken the liberty to sit down next to her, she's taking the liberty to say something that could go two completely different routes.

"So I've been told," he mutters, pulling his headphones over his head and shoving it in his bag, and Arizona remembers that boys are kind of the complete opposite of girls, and don't think much of the things she thinks too much of. Heather silently watches from beside Arizona. Jacob drains the rest of his coffee in the next few seconds, tilting his head way back to get the last drop, before he peers down, through the hole. Cursing, he sets it down at the corner of the table, and rests his chin on his palm, elbow on desk.

"You alright?" asks Arizona.

"Fine. I just really fucking hate mornings, and now I realize that I may have really taken my break year for granted. And I should really start buying large coffees." He stares bitterly at his empty, white cup. Arizona looks at him for a few more seconds, unsure what exactly she should say in this moment. He does it for her, running a hand throug his already mussed-up hair with a sigh, and tilting his head to face the girls. Jacob smiles at Heather. "And, I'm Jacob."

"Heather," she nods, with a light smile.

"I'm glad I made such a great first impression on you." Heather chuckles, leaning back in her seat.

"I think you did alright."

"I swear, I'm not like this all the time."

Arizona coughs.

"Shut up, Arizona May. I'm not."

And Arizona has to hold herself down so she doesn't throw her hands up in relief. Arizona May, Arizona May, Arizona May. Everything's alright, again.

"What?" Jacob asks, small confused smile. "Why do you look so happy?"

"I don't look happy. I'm not happy. I'm angry—I look so angry." Arizona doesn't meet Jacob's eyes, but she doesn't need to, to know that they are incredibly amused right now.

"Okay, Arizona May."

Arizona has to bite down on her lip hard to keep looking angry. She is so happy.

Thursday, September 24

Heather had steadily grown to become one of Arizona's closest friends, in the span of just a month, if not less. She enjoys many things, among which teasing Arizona about Jacob takes the cake, according to her. After the first day of Psych, as Heather and Arizona had walked back to the dorms, Heather had asked about Jacob.

"Just a friend," Arizona had said in what she hopes was a flippant manner. "I dated his brother for a while."

"And now I see why you and his brother broke up."

Arizona had looked up sharply to widen her eyes at Heather.

"What?"

"The tension between you and Jacob is tangible." After laughing at Arizona's horrified face, she had rolled her eyes. "Don't even try acting oblivious, because we both know you'd fail miserably."

"I need new friends," Arizona'd mumbled, looking at her sneakers hidding the pavement, laces bouncing up and down. She didn't know why they're so abnormally long for her shoes.

"Oh, so we're friends , now?" Heather had teased, and Arizona shot her a look.

"Were we not?"

Heather had laughed, dark eyebrows rising on her forehead like they always do when she laughs.

And now, they definitely are. Friends, that is. Arizona knows this because during Skype nights, her friends had all accused her of replacing them several times, and also because she and Heather are walking to the main road for lunch after class. Around noon the street fills with college students walking to and from class, and with the interwoven scents of different foods from the restaurants lining the asphalt. Heather had apparently found a great Mediterranean place that she wanted to try out, and who better to take than Arizona?

As the lecture ends, Arizona leans down to grab her things and picks up her bag, swinging it over her shoulder. Jacob had nearly dozed off multiple times during the lesson, and the only thing that kept him awake was Arizona's incessant poking. Arizona stands up, prodding his stretched out leg with her knee impatiently, Heather peeking out from behind her. Jacob looks at her tiredly before sighing loudly and gathering up his backpack and empty coffee cup. He taps it, a hollow sound emitting from the paper, and he jerks his arm back down to his side, muttering about how "fuckin' useless these coffee cups are." He musses up his hair and ambles out of the aisle so Arizona and Heather can scooch out. Tired Jacob is very cute.

"Where are you guys going?" he asks, yawning and stretching his arm up over his head. The day is warm today, as weird as it is, so he is in just a white t-shirt. Arizona does her best not to oggle at the thin strip of skin showing where his shirt had risen up, just above the waistband of his low-hung jeans. This is not good for her, at all, whatsoever. But, she is not complaining, either. Heather catches her and smirks. Arizona shakes her head.

"Lunch. Heather decided that today would be the day to waste hard-earned money on a fancy Mediterranean lunch, instead of perfectly delicious, yet many times questionable, streetfood. Or cereal. Those are my two choices, honestly."

Heather rolls her eyes, again—she seems to do that a lot. "It looks like a good place. And it's not that freaking fancy, get over yourself, there's only one person to take you on a date, and we all know who that is."

Arizona jabs Heather in the smug side, and Jacob looks at her questioningly. "No, we don't all know who that is. Who's she talking about, Arizona May? Got a man in your life? Boy?"

"No." Arizona grumbles, shooting a vicious glare at Heather. Jacob wiggles his eyebrows.

"Mkay."

"I do not need that tone, Jacob."

"Mka-a-ay."

"Hey, Jacob, wanna come get lunch with us?" asks Heather suddenly, and Arizona has a pressing urge to shove the girl and run.

"Uh…" Jacob looks at his phone, rubs a hand down his face and through his hair, before shrugging. "Sure, why not." The tall boy falls into step with the two others, on Arizona's right, and it takes all of her to hold herself together when their arms brush against each other multiple times. She can smell him, and wow, he smells incredible. For once in a long while, Arizona doesn't almost pass out due to too much cologne—quite the opposite, actually. Heather is saying something about something, but Arizona is completely concentrating on walking, so she doesn't trip. All this resembles a middle school crush way too much for her liking.

A couple walks by and she moves to the side to pass them, her foot consequently falling off the curb. Jacob, who had stepped completely off the sidewalk, jerks a hand out to rest on her upper arm and balance her. "Alright?" he asks with a slight smirk. Arizona narrows her eyes at him, and his smirk only grows into a smugger one. His hand sears a print on her skin, through the fabric of her t-shirt.

The three arrive at the restaurant in question after much too long, or so Arizona thinks. It's actually just a buffet, and that makes two buffets that Arizona has gone to with Jacob. She really needs to stop incorporating the boy into everything in her life. She blames it on his everpresent person.

"Smells good," he comments, stepping in behind her.

You smell good.

Arizona could swear she wasn't like this just two days ago? She doesn't know what the hell is going on with her, but it's scaring her just a little bit. She decides in this moment, the one in which Jacob has to fucking slide into a booth next to her so she gets a great freaking whiff of his scent, that she needs to get over the boy. Pining after your ex-boyfriend's brother is never a good idea, after all.

Then again, Arizona May isn't really known for her good ideas.

20

———— ◆ ————

CHAPTER 20

Priya, as it turns out, is very into the holidays. Arizona, not so much-except for Christmas. She really likes Christmas; too much, it seems, at times.

The week of Halloween, Arizona's roommate begins decorating their room, pumpkin lights strung up across the ceiling, plastic jack-o-lanterns set on the windowsills, a bowl of black and orange candy by the door, somehow always filled with the same amount, no matter how many Arizona takes every time she leaves.

Priya had been absolutely appalled when she'd heard that Arizona'd only dressed up twice in her entire life, once as a hippie when she was nine, and another time as a gumball machine in eighth grade. That Halloween had been a rough day; she wouldn't recommend that anybody dress up as a gumball machine for their costume.

"You're going to dress up," Priya had stated, shaking her head and spinning in her roll-y chair, hair tangled around pointer finger. "Our dorm and the two others near us always throw a Halloween party at our common room, since it's the biggest. It's super fun, and you're going."

And that's how Arizona winds up in the corner of the lit-up common room, clad in a pink skirt, a neon off-the-shoulder top, purple tights, huge hoop earrings, and a side ponytail. She pulls up her leg warmer so it's the same length as the other and her right hand clasps lightly around her left upper-arm. A trip to a local second-hand shop and Priya's friends' closets had scrounged up an easy 80's chick costume, which she is now kind of regretting, as she stands alone. Priya had gone to dance, but not before asking Arizona about a thousand times if she's okay being on her own for a few minutes-which Arizona convinced her that she is-but the lights seem fluorescent on Arizona's skin, which looks a sickly color against her neon clothing. Maybe she should have just gone with Katniss, or Hermione, or something. No matter the fact that she would get mistaken for another person probably a million times by the end of the night if she did.

The room is dim, the bass is pounding through the floorboards. A recognizable pop song is dissolving her, and she feels dizzy from heat and light and sound. Arizona tips the cup at her lips once more, to find that it's empty. Sighing, she kicks off the wall she had been leaning against, making her way to the drinks table. Tara is there, popping a can of soda open. The redhead smiles at Arizona, tilting the can towards her in question. Nodding, Arizona stretches her cup out, and Tara pours some Coke in.

"Having fun?" Tara asks with risen eyebrows. She's dressed in all black, a stark contrast to her fire hair, and her her leather pants cling to her mile-long legs like another layer of skin. She doesn't seem to notice all the eyes glued to her, and Arizona smiles slightly in amusement.

"Sure."

"Come on, don't be like that! Dance with us."

"You really don't want me to."

"I beg to differ."

Arizona shakes her head, laughing, and sips at her drink. Tara nudges her with her elbow.

"C'mon, it'll be fun. You'll enjoy yourself."

When Tara grabs her by the hands and pulls her to the center, where everyone dances, Arizona doesn't protest. Actually, she does, a little, but then decides that there is no point in wasting energy on trying to convince Tara of not doing something. Nobody can convince Tara to do or not do anything once she sets her mind on something. It's actually a bit scary how decisive she is.

Tara drags Arizona to the group of girls to the side of the floor, and Arizona kind of just bobs up and down uncertainly. Heather laughs and yanks Arizona to her, holding the blonde's hand above her head as she twirls under it, which doesn't quite work out due to the fact that they are in a mosh-pit, not a ballroom. Heather stumbles and Arizona straightens her out.

"I'ma lil' drunk, jussayin'." Heather puts her thumb close to her pointer finger, grinning lazily.

"Are you now."

Arizona raises her brows in amusement and Heather nods excitedly.

"In fact, I needa pee right now. Can you come with me?"

"Uhhh, no?"

"Just wait outside the door or somethin', pleeeease?" Heather pouts, a black curl falling into her eyes. Arizona sighs and shrugs, following the girl out of the crowd of dancers. At least now she has an excuse not to dance.

It takes Heather a long time in the bathroom, probably because Arizona can also hear a little bit of retching from inside. After asking if she's alright four times, Arizona sighs another long, drawn-out sigh and slides down the wall to settle on the floor, feet stretched out before her. A giggly, touchy couple stumbles down the hall, one girl's hand tangled in the other's, and Arizona quickly pulls her legs back to her chest so they don't trip over them.

She leans forward to circle her arms around her knees, resting her chin on the tops of them. A chunk of blonde falls in front of her, brushing the inside of her elbow. Arizona picks at the ends of it, studying her split-ends. She really needs to cut her hair.

"Wow, don't get too crazy. You look like you're having the time of your life."

Arizona starts and looks up with big eyes, before her heart steadies again. Well, not really, because the opposite happens whenever she sees him.

Jacob grins and sits down beside her. He's in a striped white and red shirt, and a matching hat, light wash blue jeans. "Jacob," says Arizona in greeting. "Or, should I say Waldo. Nice costume."

"Why, thank you. It took forever to put together," he says dramatically.

"I bet."

"That's a nice costume, too. What are you, that girl from Napoleon Dynamite?"

"Oh, yeah, side ponytail." Arizona grins and swishes her hair back and forth. "But, nope, just a girl from the eighties. Super fun."

Jacob peeks down at the red cup in his right hand, swishing around the drink at the bottom. He tips it towards Arizona. "I would offer you some, but sharing drinks grosses me out."

"That's okay."

"So, what's up? Why are you so...dead."

Arizona stares at Jacob.

"Not dead. Uh, why are you so-why do you look so bored out of your mind?"

"Because I'm bored out of my mind. I have this image of college parties, and I don't know, this just didn't live up to expectations. The highlight of my night is binging on free Halloween candy, honestly." Jacob raises his cup to that. "What about you? Why are you here?"

"It's really warm in there, and it's really cold outside. Just came to get a breather. Why are you right next to the bathroom, by the way?"

"Heather's inside. She made me come here. Better than dancing, though."

"You don't like dancing?" Jacob looks at her with a bewildered expression.

"I don't not like it, I just never know what to do with my hands and I just end up feeling really awkward."

"I don't see why," deadpans Jacob with a grin and Arizona elbows him.

"Was that sass."

"Yes."

"Dammit, Jacob."

He smiles cheekily. Arizona's heart stops. She hates boys. Her heart is never safe near them.

The bathroom door suddenly pulls open, and Heather stands in the doorway, coffee skin flushed, eyes tired, almond dulled as they would with age. "Parties are fun."

"Okay, Heather."

"Hey, Jacob!"

"Hey, Heather," the boy laughs a little, shoulders shaking. He is so freaking cute. And that freaking beanie and striped shirt aren't helping Arizona at all, goddammit.

After a few more minutes of Heather drunkenly saying things, she pulls Arizona up and takes her back to the common room, which is just as loud as before. This time, she stays right where she is, against the wall by the drinks table.

"You look so sad."

When Arizona looks up from her phone, a boy is leaning against the wall next to her, grin crooked and charming, black hair mussed up in a way only partying could cause. His almost eyes tilt up, and there is this happy gleam in them, an almost teasing one. A cautious one.

"Really?"

"Really. Want a refill?"

He nods towards Arizona's cup, and hesitating, she hands him the cup with a final nod.

"Thanks."

He returns it back to her, half filled with soda.

"What's your name, and why aren't you dancing? Designated driver?"

"No, I just don't want to ditch my friends. One is already drunk off her ass, and I'll probably need to get her back home."

He blinks. "So, designated driver."

"I'm not driving."

"Designated friend."

"I guess so. Goddammit."

The boy laughs, brown eyes lighting up, again.

"So? Name?"

"Arizona."

"Nice to meet you, Arizona, fellow designated driver." He sticks his hand out for her to shake, which she does.

"Friend," she corrects. "Designated friend."

"Right. Friend." He grins. "I'm Jason."

So many fucking J names. She might die from exhaustion with that letter.

It's been half an hour, when she sees Jacob, again. He is stumbling out of the crowd in the center of the room, a girl pulling him by their conjoined hands. Jacob leans against the wall adjacent to Arizona's, and the girl stands in front of him. He laughs at something she says, and she reaches up to pluck something from his hair. Arizona can only see the back of the girl's head, covered in golden hair, much different from Arizona's massive, shapeless mass the color of laundry detergent.

"Am I allowed your number?" asks Jason.

Arizona hesitates the second time with him, tonight. She bites her lip.

Jacob ducks his head a little to hear what the girl is saying, so his ear is nearly touching her lips, and he smiles, eyebrows risen. There is a drop in Arizona's stomach.

Feeling her eyes on him, Jacob suddenly looks up, too quick for Arizona to look away. So she keeps his gaze, instead, and she watches a kind smile spread across his lips. That fucking smile. It drags her in and surrounds her and drowns her, and it completely wrecks her. That fucking smile kills her.

Arizona looks back up at Jason, and nods.

"Happy Pumpkin Day, bitchachos."

"Wasn't it, like, Corpse Day or something in ninth grade?" Briana squints. Romy nods.

"Yeah, but it sounded weird, so."

"Oh, yes, just that sounded weird," sasses Crosley.

"I will actually catch a flight down there so I can personally kick your ass," glowers Romy. Gem laughs, shaking her head. The crinkling of her opening a wrapper can be heard through the speakers. "So." Romy's face pixelates and then goes back to normal as she stretches back into her chair. Her room in the background is dark, a lamp the only source of light. "When are you asking Gem out, again?"

"Shut up," mutters Gem, stuffing a Twix bar into her mouth from the square at the bottom right corner of Arizona's screen. Crosley only turns red from his square next to hers. Briana stretches her arms above her head and fixes her bun.

"Don't," says Briana. Arizona bites her lip.

"You guys-"

"I bet you ten bucks this is about Jacob," says Crosley, not unkindly. Arizona shoots him a look before shaking her head.

"You guys, I really like Jacob a whole lot."

Crosley gasps loudly, comically falling out of his chair with flailing arms before reaching up to pull himself back up again. Romy looks around her room wildly, eyes wide, mouth hanging open. Gem exclaims, "O-M-G, really?!" and Briana snorts.

"You know, you guys could be some kind of help."

"Nah," says Briana.

Arizona sighs before looking back up again. All four of her friends are looking at her, a bit worried, for the first time that night.

"Anyone with so much sugar shouldn't look that sad," says Romy, sounding genuinely concerned.

"I saw him with a girl," blurts Arizona.

"Oh," Gem purses her lip, resting her fingers on them gently as she stares at Arizona. "Are you sure she wasn't just a friend or cousin or sister or maybe even gay?"

"I'm pretty sure they were flirting."

"Babe, you-"

Crosley cuts off Briana, "Here's what you're going to do. Stop messing around with him. Next time you see him, you're going to shove him against a wall and kiss him and maybe do the dirty, and then you'll get him out of your system, and you'll never want to get with him again. I bet all this is about you wanting to fuck him, anyway."

Arizona stares at Crosley. "Aren't you a virgin?"

He glares at her, hard, and Gem laughs. Crosley flushes.

"Whatever, I'm not doing that. Any other tips?"

Crosley ends up sulking for the next few minutes, but by the time the fourth minute has passed, he's forgotten what he'd been sulking about, in the first place, and continues interjecting with other sexual suggestions.

"Seriously, what's wrong with you," says Romy, picking at her fingernails.

"I need more candy, that's what's wrong." Crosley holds up an empty, orange, plastic bowl. "Bee-are-bee."

"Don't say that," mumbles Briana, resting her chin in her palm. Ignoring her, he jumps off his chair and runs out the door. A second later he pops back into the room, bowl still empty.

"Forgot my pants," he clicks his tongue and tugs a pair of shorts over his boxers before leaving again.

"Dammit," says Briana. "It would've been funny if he never remembered."

"True," says Gem.

"Don't pretend, Gem, we all know that's not why you don't want him wearing any pants."

Gem's square turns black and disappears.

21

—— ● ——

CHAPTER 21

Arizona had been nervous about landing, because maybe she wouldn't be able to find her family, but when she does walk through the PDX Airport, she realizes that there was no sense in that aprehension, because the first thing she sees is her mother's blonde bob bouncing up and down, hand waving frantically around her head. There is a blinding, excited grin on Cora's face as she keeps flailing her hands-even though she knows Arizona's seen-much to the distress of those surrounding her. Arizona's father stands a little behind his wife, one hand in a pocket, the other holding his phone up, his face tilted down at it. But, when he looks up and sees Arizona, an almost identical smile breaks onto his face.

Her suitcase catches on her heel, and Arizona stumbles. She straightens back up, smiling sheepishly at the elderly man who had been reaching out to help her. She mumbles a thank you to him before trying to walk to where her parents stand, in the most dignified manner possible.

Cora jumps on Arizona, first, pumping the breath out of the girl as she hugs her so tightly Arizona thinks she may burst. Her dad gives her a simple slap on the back, which doesn't really help much, either, because his light pat amounts to ten bricks falling on her.

He's a skinny man, so everything he does, he does to make up for the lack of bulk.

"I brought you guys matching key rings," grins Arizona, pulling the souvenirs from her backpack's front pocket. It's a simple, silver Statue of Liberty, but her mother's eyes light up immediately with excitement, and her father smiles, slipping it onto his keys already. He pats her on the shoulder, again. Arizona bites her tongue.

"Thanks so much, Zona, these are so cute!" Cora gushes.

When they reach their home, the two lights next to the garage are on. "Lara and Ross are home," explains Ben. Arizona lets out a breath and nods. She hasn't seen Lara in months, she can do this. She can last five days.

They enter through the garage, and before Cora can call her older daughter down, Arizona runs down the stairs to her room. The door slams open and she welcomes the sight and scent of the books like an old friend. She's missed her room. Sighing, Arizona allows her things to fall to the ground by her closet, before collapsing face-forward on her bed.

She lies prostate for about an hour more, dipping in and out of sleep, before her mother calls for dinner. It's nice, not having to trudge up to the food court, or not being forced to find a cheap microwave dinner at her local, overpriced grocery store. She actually has no idea why they would put such an expensive place in the middle of a college campus, of all the places in the world.

When Arizona walks into the kitchen, Cora is bustling around the counter, tasting something from a pot. Ross is at the dinner table, working on something on his laptop. He looks up and sees Arizona, grinning in greeting. She high-fives his risen hand before sitting down in a chair on the other side of the dinner table..

"How's the college life?" Ross settles back in his chair, shutting his laptop.

"It's alright, actually. Either it's super fun, or super stressful."

Laughing, he tilts his head in agreement.

"That's true."

"Wait, what was your degree, again?" Arizona peers at him.

"Programming."

"Oh." Arizona's eyebrows rise. "Wow."

"It's not the most interesting, but, I mean, money, right?"

Laughing, she nods. Right.

Lara pads in a second later, eyes tired, hair down. She's in a sweatshirt and pajama pants, and Arizona is a little bewildered. This is the last outfit she'd have expected of her older sister.

"Hey, welcome back," Lara smiles warmly, and Arizona is actually speechless.

Carefully, she says, "Hey. Thanks."

Lara sits down next to Ross. Her eyes seem faded; less dark, less alluring. She's not wearing make-up. She's still freaking gorgeous.

"How's NYU?" asks Lara, with a weary politeness sinking her words. Arizona's parents come to sit down with them, a pot of carrot soup in the center of the table, a glass bowl of salad and a plate of bread next to it.

"It's alright. College is fun."

"Yeah, it is."

Maybe all this pettiness between Lara and Arizona is finally over. And, yes, Arizona admits she only added fuel to the fire.

After dinner, Arizona walks to Briana's house, where everyone is supposed to meet up. The front door is open when Arizona checks, and she walks in quietly, stacking her shoes with the other next to the wall adjacent to the door. She can hear voices in the kitchen, but they sound like adults, so holding her breath, she slips up the carpeted stairs as silently as her socked feet take her, and when she bursts through Briana's door, Crosley screams and falls over, rolling out from behind the door in a fetal position. Arizona blinks at him blankly and Gem grins.

"It's the squad!"

"Don't call us that, Romy," snaps Crosley, but nobody can take him seriously when he is on his side, legs pressed to his chest, hand cradled in his other.

"What happened to you?" asks Arizona.

"The door you just fucking opened just fucking god my fingers stuck under it and it fucking hurt, is what fucking happened!" he cries, and Arizona gently nudges him with her foot before sitting on the floor next to Romy.

"I've missed us," sighs Briana, small smile on her face, once she sits back from giving Arizona a hug.

"Have you? Really?" Crosley squints and Gem kicks him from where she sits on the bed.

"Shut up, Cros, you have too. You know you have."

He smacks her foot away from his face, but everybody sees the tiny smile just barely tilting his lips.

"Whatever."

Thursday, November 26

When Cora asks whether Arizona wants to invite Jeremy over for Thanksgiving dinner, Arizona decides to push back the date for telling her mom they've broken up. She'd rather not tell her mom that since Arizona's started college, she's actually lost a boy.

Now, Arizona is in the kitchen, doing her homework at the table. She is the only one in there, and she is supposed to keep an eye on the turkey. But, apparently it's not supposed to smell like burnt toast, because the next second, the smoke detector goes off, the annoying, high-pitched beeping cutting through her throughts. Cora comes running, yelping and waving her arms around frantically.

"Zona, you were supposed to keep an eye on the turkey!" she says, tone incredibly annoyed as she opens all the windows at record speed. She yanks the oven door open and orders for Arizona to get the meat out, and Cora grabs two pans, waving them around rapidly around the kitchen, trying to get rid of the smoke. "Ben!"

Panicked, Arizona takes the pan out of the oven, realizing only too late that she's forgotten her mitts. Cursing loudly (and making sure to avoid any eye contact with her mother when doing so) she slams it down onto the stove, hissing in pain and shoving her hands under the cold faucet water.

"One thing, Arizona," Lara rolls her eyes, swishing into the kitchen-because that is literally how she walks. She swishes. "You were in charge of one thing." Arizona glares at her, and the smoke detector finally shuts off, and Cora finally seems able to breathe.

"Swear to God, this happens every year," mumbles Ben, walking into the kitchen with a bland look.

"Just cut off the burnt parts," says Arizona, and Cora turns to stare at her incredulously.

"No, you just cut off the burnt parts." She hands a serrated knife to Arizona, who takes it cautiously, in case her mother decides to commit one last violent act.

Every year.

An hour later, the family is finally sat around the dinner table, and Arizona is well aware of the fact that if this dinner were to be called a disaster-which no one has, mind you-the fault would be on her. Picking her fork up, she jabs a piece of turkey sans skin onto the end of it, and dips it into the sauce.

"Wait, wait, don't eat yet!"

Arizona sighs and her fork clatters to her plate. Cora's eyes are wide and excited.

"We have to give our thanks."

Sighing again, arizona gets up with everybody else, and they form a small circle in the kitchen, holding hands with one another.

Cora is grateful for her family and for shelter and for food. Ben is grateful for what cora is grateful for. Arizona is grateful for everything her parents are grateful for. Lara is grateful for her family and for shelter and for food and for ross, and Ross is grateful for everything and for his wife.

"What?" blinks Lara.

And then Ross gets down on his knee, and he is fumbling for something in his pocket, and Arizona is gaping, and Cora is squeaking, and Ben is clapping a hand over his wife's mouth to shush her, and Lara is clapping a hand over her mouth. Ross is completely flushed, much different from his usual cool exterior, and he pulls out a tiny, velvet box, flipping it open in his hand. Arizona's forgotten about her slightly burnt fingers.

"I know you've always wanted some big, cute proposal, and believe me when I say that this is the best way I could think of proposing, and I have no idea if you wanted it with your family there, but I don't care, as long as it means that you might say yes, and you might become my wife. I love you so much, and I think you're the most incredible person I have ever met, the most beautiful human I have ever come to know, and it would really, really, really, making me very freaking happy, if you would do me the honor of marrying me." He says it fast and eloquently, in one breath, as if he's practiced it over and over and over again in front of a mirror until his throat got sore and his breaths got hitched.

Arizona doesn't even have enough words to think snarky thoughts to herself, about the things he had said about Lara, because somebody is proposing to her sister in a very cute fucking manner, and Arizona might not be the number one fan of her older sister, but she is a second away from lunging at Lara and moving her mouth to say yes.

Arizona's sister might be crying-something Arizona doesn't think she has ever seen in her entire existence, and then Lara is leaning down, but Ross is getting back up and she is hugging him, and Lara doesn't even have to say it for ross to know that she will marry him, because she is hugging him so tight, and because they love each other so much.

And, shit. Arizona wants it. She wants that so bad it hurts.

Friday, November 27

Arizona enjoys the presence of Fiance-Lara more than she had that of Girlfriend-Lara. Fiance-Lara is kinder, and more interesting to talk to, and Arizona actually really likes Fiance-Lara. She doesn't even mind when Fiance-Lara does everything she can to wave her hand around so everybody in a ten mile radius can get a glimpse at the rock on her ring finger. Ross thinks it's adorable.

The ring is very pretty, though. It's diamond, and shaped like a little heart, with gold looping around it to twist in the middle of the stone, and the band is gold.

Now, she is out Black Friday shopping with Lara (Fiance-Lara) and Ross, though Ross had disappeared on them halfway through the mall when he'd seen a Brookstone. There are about fifty hangers draped over Lara's arm, and about one hundred draped all over Arizona, as she trails behind the older girl, too tired to protest. Plus, Lara had promised to buy Arizona anything she wants from here, as long as it's cute. Fiance-Lara is very loose with her money. Arizona likes that.

Hours later, the two collapse in the food court, Lara with four bags-less than Arizona'd thought there'd be-and Arizona with two. She'd recognized many old classmates from Washington High, and laughing, Lara had helped Arizona hide from them. Arizona hates seeing school people outside of school. It's very disorienting. And, it also doesn't help that Arizona is in her finest pair of sweats at three a.m.

"Arizona, I'm getting married."

Lara keeps picking up her pretzel to take a bite before setting it back down when a huge grin takes over her lips.

"I'm aware of that. Do you know when? Or where?"

"Nope."

"Oh."

"But, I don't care, because...oh, my God!" Lara waves her ringed-hand around ecstatically, and Arizona jerks her head back before getting smacked in the face. From the corner of her eye she sees a man catching sight of Lara's engagement ring and looking away with a disgruntled expression. Arizona bites her lip in amusement.

"Lara, do you realize that you won't be able to date anymore?"

"I don't care, Arizona!"

And Arizona smiles, because she finally actually really likes Lara.

22

Chapter 22

Arizona's diet used to consist of ramen bowls. It's the week before finals. Now, her diet consists of a coffee and pretzels. She swears she's lost weight again. So much for freshman fifteen, it's probably become something like freshman negative forty, by now. Every day she discovers a new pimple on her forehead, and she hasn't watched a sitcom in what feels like forever. She doesn't think she'd be able to sit and be calm, anyway.

Every night, Cora video chats Arizona to fret about, worrying about whether her daughter's eaten, yet—"Yes" (see: no)—and whether she's okay there, on her own—"I miss you guys" (see: but I fucking love living on my own).

Arizona had run into Jacob at the grocery one night, when she'd been picking up a package of coffee. She's blurted out that she'd been having trouble, and asked if he'd like to study with her. He'd said yes. Arizona's chest was a drum. They'd decided to meet at the campus library at eight, after dinner, on Saturday night.

Later, she'd seen him kissing a girl in aisle seven, and Arizona had recognized the perfectly golden tresses. The girl had been in sweats and a tight sweater, and Arizona knew that if you kissed in the middle of aisles and went late-night grocery shopping together in your sweats, there was just one label you could put on your relationship.

Now, she shifts around, adjusting the bag's strap looped over her shoulder, and the holder of coffees in her right hand. She said she would bring coffee, so she brought coffee. She struggles for a second, trying to get a hold of the doorknob with all the textbooks and hot drinks in her hands. Letting out a breath when the door unlatches, Arizona turns to push against it, and she stumbles in. Jacob said he would be on the second level, near the back of the room, where there are long, mahogany tables. There are a few students sitting around, two talking in hushed voices, everybody else totally concentrated on textbooks and laptops.

Jacob isn't here, yet, so Arizona sets her things down on an empty table, flicking the lamp close to her on. There are a lot of windows in the library, and she can see the winter outside, at the white everything. Unzipping her jacket, she drapes it over the back of her chair and untangles the scarf from her neck, putting it down beside her. There are dark splotches on her jeans, where snow had melted, and her face is probably all red from the cold.

Arizona stares outside for a few minutes before blinking herself out of the reverie and starting up her laptop. Her fingers tap on the desk as she waits for it to launch. Her hands fly up to her face, and she finds her face tired under her fingerpads, thumbs sinking into dark circles, index fingers running over small bumps. She's completely void of makeup today, and is regretting it, because now Jacob will see this. But, when he sits down across from her a minute later, he looks at her no different, and Arizona soon forgets about her lack of makeup.

"Hey," he smiles at her, sliding his laptop out from his satchel. His nose is pink, and his hair is mussed, little pieces of snow still stuck to it. Arizona bites down on her lips, hard.

"Hi."

Jacob's eyes flit to the lone coffee left in the cardboard holder.

"Oh, is this for me?"

"Yeah, I...yeah."

"Thanks."

"Sure."

Arizona swallows and looks back at her keyboard.

"So." Jacob sips at his coffee and puts it down again, before sliding his black jacket off. He's wearing a gray waffle shirt underneath, and it clings to his chest so perfectly Arizona might throw up. "What do you want to start with?"

"Psych?" she laughs, and he grins, shrugging.

"Sounds good."

Groaning in frustration, Arizona slams her pencil down onto her notebook.

"I don't understand why we need to memorize so much vocabulary to understand how a person's mind works! I just—I—no!"

Grinning, Jacob puts the flashcards down, reclining back into his chair. Arizona glares at them, and he tips the cup at his mouth, frowning slightly when he finds it empty.

"Want to get more coffee? A break?"

"Yes, please. No one will steal our stuff at nine at night at the library, right?"

"No," Jacob rolls his eyes.

"Okay, just asking. Jeez." It's stopped snowing, now, but the cold still nips at her ears, and her nose tingles, as if on the brink of a sneeze. Jacob rubs at the slight stubble growing on his cheek, before tucking both hands into his pockets. Arizona swallows, pulling her eyes away to the streetlamp. The sky is pink, reflecting off the blanket of white snow, and she steps in clean patches to hear the crunch of her boot sinking in it. "Ross proposed to my sister," she says after a second. Jacob's eyebrows rise.

"And she said yes? I thought you said she has commitment is-sues."

"I'm just as surprised as you," Arizona smiles and shrugs.

"That's great, though."

She hums, nodding.

"What's your favorite season?" Jacob asks randomly, kicking some white dust up at his feet. He steps carefully, watching his footprints left behind.

"Winter. And I appreciate this New York snow, I really do, but—I can't believe I'm saying this—it's getting very tiring. Like, it's pretty from inside, you know what I'm saying?"

"Yeah. Like rain. I like winter, too. But Spring is the best, I think. Everything looks better in Spring."

"Ugh, but that's when all the sandals and gross feet come out."

"You mean with the socks?"

"Don't even talk about socks and sandals."

Jacob laughs, and Arizona nearly trips, it's such a beautiful thing. If winter were a sound, it would be his laugh.

"What's your...favorite color?"

Jacob crinkles his brows, dropping his pencil on the desk and rubbing his forehead. "I don't have one. I prefer muted colors when it comes to buying stuff, though. If that counts."

"It doesn't."

"Okay, well I don't actually give a shit, so."

"Rude."

"Favorite place."

"My room. You?" Arizona pauses in her writing to glance up at him briefly. His eyes are trained on his screen, flying from side to side.

"There's this avenue downtown, and there's a lot of cool places, like a bookstore and a café and a noodle place, and this burger place that has the best fries, and this ice-cream place and—"

"You could have just stopped."

"I'm sorry." Jacob's tongue flicks out and slides over his bottom lip. Arizona nearly passes out. "I'm not the best at multi-tasking."

"What? Really?"

"I honestly don't appreciate that."

"Sorry," mutters Arizona.

"Apology not accepted."

"Dickweed."

"Wait—Jacob, when's your birthday?"

Arizona had suddenly bene hit with the realization that she doesn't know when this boy's birthday is. Maybe he'd mentioned it, but she sure does not remember.

"December 13."

Arizona blinks.

"That's tomorrow."

"I am aware," he grins a tired grin. They are the only two in the library, now, so they don't have to be totally quiet, anymore. The lamps are luminous and warm, spilling gold everywhere, and it almost makes Arizona want to fall asleep. Jacob's eyes fall to his phone that had just lit up with a text. He doesn't answer it, but he does look up to meet her gaze. "In less than an hour, actually."

"What the fuck, Jacob."

"What?"

"You can't just do that. You can't just not tell me about your birthday until an hour before."

"You never asked," he grins cheekily.

Arizona rolls her eyes.

"So, you have a girlfriend, now, huh?"

Jacob coughs, putting his cup of coffee back down. He watches her with a calculating look, fingers fiddling with the frayed edges of his textbook.

"Yes."

"That's nice. She seems nice."

Arizona has never spoken to her, only seen her twice—once at the Halloween party, and once at the grocery. Jacob knows this. He doesn't comment on it, though.

"She is," he says, instead.

Arizona wants to chuck her Psych textbook at her pretty little head. She purses her lips into a smile, looking down.

"Where'd you meet her?"

"In the plaza. I was studying. She started talking to me."

"Ah."

Arizona can't breathe, she can't breath, why can't she breathe?

"Why?" asks Jacob, tilting his head in an adorably infuriating manner.

"What?"

"Why do you ask?"

"Oh." Arizona laughs a little, waving her hand around in a way she hopes is flippant. "There's no reason. Just asking about you, your life. Why would something be wrong?"

"Gee, I dunno, maybe because you haven't asked what her name is."

"Wow, okay, Sherlock," she rolls her eyes, annoyance slipping into her tone. His eyebrows rise.

"Whoa, what did I do now?"

"Nothing. You did absolutely nothing," she says, but it sounds like she spits it, because this uncontrollable anger is rising in her. What is wrong with her?

"Arizona, seriously."

May. Arizona May.

"What is it, did I say something wrong?" Jacob looks genuinely confused, and Arizona hates that she's reacting this way because the night had been going just so well, and she is just ruining every-thing, and because no, Jacob didn't say anything wrong, and if there ever really was something between them, this would surely be the end.

"No."

"Then why are you so mad at me?"

"I'm not mad at you!" she exclaims suddenly, standing up, hair fly-ing up into her face. Jacob reclines back in his chair, bewildered face melting into a slightly annoyed one. "I'm mad at myself! Because I didn't do anything! I didn't do anything at all! And now you have a girlfriend, and it's killing me!" Her voice seems big and heavy and looming in the dark library. It doesn't echo, but it falls short. Jacob stares at her for a second before a look of realization falls onto his face, and then there is this scalding glint in his eye.

"Whoa, wait, are you kidding me, right now? Are you jealous?" He looks completely pissed, now, something Arizona is never seen before, ever. He has always been calm and cool, never angry. Arizona doesn't say anything. "We had a deal," he says, eyes narrow. "We would stay away from each other, because if you don't remember, you dated my brother for months. You kissed me after those months, okay? You kissed me. You said, "maybe we shouldn't spend so much time together." And I said yes. But, turns out, that doesn't work out very well, because we're spending so much time together, and now I have a girlfriend, and you can't handle that, apparently."

His voice is low, and he doesn't yell, but the way he says his words is about a thousand times scarier than if he had.

"I'm keeping up my end of the bargain. I'm not making any moves. But, God forbid, I go out with somebody else! God forbid I don't kiss you. Remember that time you told Jeremy you kissed me? And he told you it was fine? It wasn't. it killed him. He didn't speak to me for a week. And I don't know what it's like you with your sister, because let's face it, you guys don't exactly have the best fucking relationship in the world, but Jeremy and I are friends, he's the one person I can always count on, no matter how much of a douchebag he may be. I can't hurt him like that, not again." Jacob's voice has just become hard, barely angry. "And don't think I didn't see you talking to Jason."

Arizona throws her hands up in exhasperation. Of course.

"You know Jason?"

"He's my roommate."

"You've got to be kidding me."

Jacob stares at her, she clenches her jaw. She hates this. When had her life become one of her mom's television dramas? "You guys dating?" Like a flipped switch, he says it cooly, casually, as he slides back into his seat and rests his chin in his palm, eyes trained on the textbook before him.

"I—I, uh, no—uh, no."

He looks up and raises a brow at her. Arizona pushes her glasses up her nose, sitting down, as well.

"We're going on a date next week."

"Cool. Where?" He only glances at her for a split-second. He doesn't care. He's asking out of courtesy. Arizona is sad.

"We're going to that oldie cinema on the main road. The small one."

"Sounds fun," he says. Arizona squeezes her eyes shut for a few seconds before opening them again and starting on the next paragraph. She reads the thesis four times, five times, six times. She still doesn't know what it says. The tense, tangible silence between them lasts for ten more minutes, until Arizona clears her throat and stands up abruptly.

"Right. So, I don't think I can study anymore." At this he smirks, because he knows they haven't studied anything at all, basically. She gathers her things up hurriedly, itching to leave this library. "See you...around?"

Jacob gives her a short, clipped nod. Arizona walks out of the library, the only sound from behind her is the scratch of a pencil against paper. Before she shuts the heavy door, she hears a faint "Good night." There is a fist lodged in Arizona's throat.

Arizona clicks her phone on, and the four numbers glaring back at her stab at her like a million knives. 12:04 a.m. December 13.

23

CHAPTER 23

Arizona had sat in a different seat for the first time the entire year, in Psych. Always the loyal friend, Heather had plopped down next to her. Jacob had seemed a bit bothered as he watched her travel across the room to sit on the other side from him, but he'd just fallen asleep later one, as per usual. Arizona made sure to bite back any smiles that threatened to rise up onto her face.

Today, Jason takes her out on the date he'd promised her when he'd called her two weeks ago. Arizona hadn't thought that he would; she'd thought that he'd just been one of those boys who saw a girl and asked for their number, just to have something to do, but never actually called despite any promises they made.

Priya flings a yellow dress onto the bed, next to Arizona, without looking. She continues rumaging through the closet as Arizona picks up the aforementioned dress. It's cute, with three-quarter sleeves and a skirt that would just skim her knees. Her eyebrows rise.

"He won't be able to tell where my hair stops and the dress starts," she comments, and Priya's laugh is muffled amongst the clothes. "Also, might I point out that it is late winter and freezing and snowing outside?"

"Wear it with tights and a scarf and cardigan. And if you put your hair up, it won't be a problem. It doesn't even look like the same color as your dress," Priya rolls her eyes, and Arizona grins. Jason said that he'd pick her up in front of the dorms. She quickly dresses in what Priya had said, and slips into a pair of tall boots before grabbing her bag from the hook by her bed. With a quick hug, Arizona is out of the door and padding down the hall, opting to take the stairs over the elevator. She hasn't gone on a date in forever—in fact, the last one was with Jeremy nearly a year ago. She thinks that if she goes in the elevator, she will be forced to feel nervous about all this. And she will be forced to think about Jacob, whom she hasn't spoken to in a week, but she thinks that that may be more her fault than his. Whenever she saw him in the food court or the plaza, she'd made sure to go any other way. There had been only one instance where where there was no way out, and she had just smiled at him briefly before walking away.

Arizona waits outside for two minutes before she sees Jason walking towards her. It's not snowing, but she knows that it has stopped only briefly. she blows into her cupped hands, rubbing them together. As he approaches her and comes to a halt before Arizona, Jason grins and flicks some hair out of his eyes. His hair is much blacker than Jacob's, whose looks brown in the sunlight. Fuck, she needs to stop attaching Jacob to every single thought she has.

"Hey," he says, hands tucked into his tan coat's pockets. "You look nice."

"Thanks, so do you," Arizona smiles, albeit a bit shyly.

"So, there's this super cool sushi place downtown that I thought you might like. Rumor has it that it's very sustainable, too, so, you know. Save the environment and stuff." He shoots Arizona a cheesy grin, and she laughs, nodding.

"That sounds great."

They start off on the sidewalk, and multiple times Arizona nearly slips and falls, and multiple times Jason steadies her. Multiple times Arizona is aware of her heart, which isn't attempting to beat out of her heart, unlike the state it is in whenever she's with a different boy. Arizona wants to dump a handful of snow down her back, because maybe that will wake her up from this boy-filled gray zone of conflict. She may go insane, if she doesn't soon.

"You alright?" asks Jason kindly, peering at her from the corner of his eye. Arizona shoots him a quick, easy smile.

"Yeah. I just didn't...think that you would actually call."

"Really."

"Yeah."

"You seemed very cool. Plus, like, y'know, your face...is very interesting."

"Interesting." Arizona raises her brows. He chuckles, scratching the back of his neck awkwardly.

"Yeah. Like...what's your ethnicity?"

Arizona stifles a smile.

"Japanese-American. No one really gets my blonde hair, me included."

"Hey, I'm Japanese!"

"Wow, so cool!" Arizona makes her eyes big and glues on an astounded smile.

"That was too sarcastic for my liking," Jason mumbles.

"Sorry."

"No, you're not."

"No, I'm not."

Halfway through their dinner, Jason sets down his chopsticks and folds his arms on the table, staring straight at Arizona. Blinking, she does the same, amused smile kissing her lips.

"I like talking to you," says Jason.

"Well, I like talking to you, too."

"But, I have a question."

"Fire away."

"Do you..." Jason glances down at his napkin before looking at her with squinted eyes, "...want to stay just friends?"

Arizona's reply comes immediately, with no hesitation, "Yes, please."

"I don't know whether to be offended or not, with how fast that response came," he laughs lightly.

"You should definitely be offended. I hate you, tonight has been terrible."

"You weren't so sarcastic at the party, back when I thought you were a nice person." Arizona grins cheekily. "Rude."

"Only to my friends."

At that, Jason smiles.

It's late December, when Arizona sits straight up in bed in the middle of the day, hit with the sudden realization that she goes back home for the holidays in a few days, and still hasn't gotten Christmas presents for anyone, except this pair of socks she found and thought Briana would like. The girl has a concerningly large sock collection.

Priya is out with her friends, and Arizona'd been planning on spending a lazy day in her pajamas and in bed with a book and tea. She hasn't read a novel in nearly five months. And now, it seems like December will just add one more month to that, because she had so stupidly forgotten about presents. With a sigh, Arizona flips the duvet cover off of her plaid-clad legs, and swings around to stand up and find something presentable to wear in her closet. It's been even colder lately, which, yes, is possible, apparently. She slips her arms into a thick fleece, pulls on a hat, knots a scarf around her kneck, and tugs on her boots.

It's five o'clock when she shuts the door to her room. She checks everything in her bag, again, as she walks down the hall, and when she looks up, she's running into something—or somebody. A somebody that smells suspiciously familiar. Suspiciously delicious. Dammit. Arizona's hat had fallen off when they'd crashed, and wincing, she leans down to retrieve it, because she'd do anything to delay looking him in the eye.

Unfortunately, he decides to lean down at the same time, and her head knocks into his. Cursing, she scoots back awkwardly, finally looking at him, hand wrapped around her other elbow. He seems to bite back his own string of profanities. Jacob smiles smally and asks, "You alright?" Arizona laughs shortly and nods, biting her lip. The air is tense between them. She hasn't really spoken to him since his birthday. Nothing except fleeting greetings when they ran into each other in Teacup or the grocery. Arizona hadn't braced herself for an interaction so soon.

"Yeah. Uh—" she makes a move to get her hat, again, but Jacob interrupts her.

"I'll get it. Don't duck down," he says, only slightly joking, and Arizona doesn't. He returns the hat to her, and sets it on her head, pulling it over her (now red) ears. His fingers skim her cheeks and Arizona stifles a sigh.

"Oh," she says, instead, because that's really all she can say.

He smiles, eyes crinkling in that totally unfairly endearing way. "Where are you off to in the cold?"

"I procrastinated on getting Christmas presents."

"You're getting them from here? But extra tax?"

"I'll just get them small things. You know, from New York and stuff. Souvenirs, maybe."

They stand in the hall for a few moments, the odd person walking past, mumbling an excuse me to get past. Arizona plays with her fingers before shoving her hands deep into her pockets. Jacob scratches the back of his neck in a manner much more attractive than that of Jason's.

"Do...uh, do you wanna come? With me? Do you need to buy anything?" Arizona's words stumble out, and she hadn't meant to say them, but now it's too late, and all she can do is stare at him and wait for the answer expectantly.

"Oh, uh, no, we don't celebrate."

Arizona crooks an eyebrow.

"I'm Jewish."

"Huh. I didn't know that."

"And now you do."

She grins, "Do you want to come, anyway?"

Jacob looks down the hall, scratching the back of his neck, again, and then mussing up his hair before looking back down at Arizona. "I...sure, why not."

Despite the snow and relatively late hour, there's a lot of people at the mall. Only a portion is college students, some highschoolers and families ambling around. Half an hour into shopping, and Jacob had declared his hunger. Now, they are waiting in a ridiculously long line in front of the pretzel booth.

They stand beside each other, Arizona only now realizing just how much shorter she is than him. Jacob seems to have noticed the difference in their heights, too, because he mumbles that she's short, and she elbows him, retracting her arm a second later with a clear of her throat. She's not sure if they're friends again, yet.

"I'm sorry," says Arizona, breaking the silence. She doesn't ask for his apology and he doesn't give one. He doesn't even owe her one, anyway. Everything he had said that night had been completely true, and Arizona wishes it isn't like that, but it is. Jacob glances at her, licks his lips, and nods once.

"It's alright. I may have overreacted."

"Not really."

The two step up to the register, and Jacob rattles off an order for the both of them, and Arizona slips her five dollar bill across the counter so quickly that he doesn't get the chance to protest. She just knows that he's the type to pay oh so chivalrously, because Jacob is fucking perfect. Grinning smugly at him, she takes the pretzel and bites it. He rolls his eyes back, not unkindly.

Jacob and Arizona make their way around a group of giggling girls and a very red-in-the-face boy, to a little shop with cute cards and stuffed animals in the window. She starts shuffling through stacks of t-shirts and hats.

"Are you still with..."

Arizona bites her tongue, realizing too late that she still doesn't know her name.

"Melanie?" he offers, the left side of his lips tilting up in faint amusement.

"Right, Melanie. Are you guys still dating?"

"Nah..." Jacob takes a bite of his pretzel and plays with a tiny snowglobe of Rockefeller Center, "...we broke up when she made it clear that she didn't really want a relationship relationship. She just wanted the slice of this." He gestures down at his body, wiggling his eyebrows, a sarcastic and slightly bitter smile twisting his mouth. Arizona snorts, back of her throat stinging now. She coughs and Jacob pats her back gently with a bewildered look. She waves him away.

"Don't ever say that, again."

"Never?"

"Never."

"Okay."

Arizona checks the price tag of a graphic tee with a skateboarding cat on the front. Crosley loves cats.

"Not even whe—"

"Never, Jacob."

Jacob makes big eyes at her, an exaggerated offended look on his face as he walks away to the cards section with a wave of his hand. Arizona smiles and shakes her head. She likes him so much, it isn't even funny anymore.

"Did you buy tickets to go back home for winter break?"

Jacob looks up from the keychain he'd been turning around in his hands. "Not yet. You wanna get the same flight?"

Arizona raises her eyebrows in surprise. Man, he forgives easily. It almost makes her feel guilty about that time she didn't speak to Crosley for three days in seventh grade because he told her that she dances like a flamingo ("I don't think flamingos can really dance, Crosley." "Exactly, dipshit." "I hope you know that you're actually the worst."). "Yeah, that'd be great."

"I can just buy both of ours and you can pay me back."

"Okay. yeah."

"Okay." he smiles at her before flipping a bowler onto his head.

"Oh, my God, take that off." Arizona laughs and he raises a brow at her and it is not at all terribly sexy, of course not. Arizona wants to groan in exasperation, she's so mad at herself for liking him so much.

Jacob pulls an irritatingly cute apalled face. "Take what off?"

"The hat, Jacob. The hat, goddammit."

Arizona is no doubt red. Didn't take Jacob long at all.

24

— ◆ —

CHAPTER 24

All Arizona can think about is Christmas and Jacob. Now, as she finishes up packing her clothing, she is beginning to question whether getting the same flight as Jacob had been a good idea. She's a little bit afraid that she'll end up throwing up on the airplane, she likes him so much.

Priya had left for home in the morning, and Arizona's flight is at three in the afternoon. Just as she zips up her bag, there are two knocks on the door and a muffled announcement of "Open up, it's the police." Rolling her eyes, Arizona yanks the door open to find Jacob standing with a risen fist and a goofy grin she wants to kiss off his face, in all honesty. A black suitcase stands upright next to him and Arizona raises her brows at him in greeting before retreating back into the room. She keeps the door open for him, and he follows her in. It feels intimate, with him in her room. He's never seen it before—not even her bedroom back home.

When she turns back around, Jacob is staring at the portraid that James had done of her, which she'd placed in the windowsill. The side of his lip tilts up in the amused way that hurts Arizona's heart.

"Dear God, he's in deep," Jacob murmers, and Arizona frowns.

"What?"

"James drew that, right?" Arizona nods. Jacob laughs and tilts his head slightly. "He has such a crush on you." Arizona flushes.

"He does not!"

"Yes. He does."

"Whatever."

She jerks the suitcase off her bed and marches out the door. Jacob's laugh follows her down the narrow hall to the elevator. She wants to bottle up that stupid laugh and keep it by her bed.

As the Oregonians they are, the two had decided to just take the same cab, because it would save many things—in which her heart does not take part. The plan to avoid each other has really gone down the toilet, and Arizona can't say with complete honest that she totally regrets it.

Arizona likes airports, a lot. Everything and everyone is temporary, except for the little shops and restaurants, that are always there whenever she comes. She likes the smell, of carpet cleaner and luggage, and she likes how everyone is wearing different clothes, because some are in shorts and tanktops, ready to go to Australia, and other's are in thick sweaters and sweatpants, bundling up for Alaska. She likes how nobody knows anybody, and it doesn't matter, either, because everybody leaves eventually.

After checking in their baggage, they have an hour to spend until boarding. Jacob starts over to the coffee shop, and Arizona drifts to the little bookstore. It smells so good inside, like old books and paper, that she almost passes out.

She likes the memoir section the most, because the lives of comedians almost always prove to be more interesting than hers. Jacob appears beside her suddenly, sipping from a white, capped cup, another held in his left hand. He offers to Arizona, to takes it with a thanks. Her hands cup around it, and the smell of coffee and Christmas wafts up to her nose in curls of smoke.

"Whatchoo doing?"

"What does it look like."

He hipchecks her before grabbing a book at random and flipping it over to read the back cover.

"You really like reading," he comments, not looking at her. Arizona shrugs.

"Yeah, I do."

"Teach me your ways."

"You don't like reading?"

"I mean, I don't love it."

"Oooh, hold on, I'll find you a book that you'll love."

"I'm sure you will."

"You'll fall so in love with reading because of this one totally weird, magnificently hipster book." Arizona grabs the first book that she sees that she recognizes. As it happens, she never finished the book.

"Is that so?" Jacob arches a dubious brow and Arizona nods. "Tell me. The Joke Milan Kundera writes about—is it you?"

"Ha-ha." Arizona smacks the aforementioned novel into his chest with an unamused expression. Jacob shoots her an irresistably boyish grin.

"What is the joke, then?"

"That's for you to find out," Arizona says in what she hopes is a mysterious manner.

"You've never read it, have you," smirks Jacob, glancing down at the cover.

"Yes I have!"

"Finished it?"

"Nope."

"Ah."

Boarding starts at 5:25, and Arizona and Jacob are already sat in their seats, beside each other. They had actually been placed in rows in front of one another, but Jacob had deemed that unacceptable and asked to switch with the person beside Arizona. Now he sits with his limbs splayed out everywhere, and his arm brushes against hers. She strungles for every breath. The person behind her kicks Arizona's seat and she bites her lip. Dammit, she hates kickers.

The plane is freezing, and apparently the three feet of New York snow outside hadn't been enough for the captain to turn on the heat. "What the fuck," she hisses now, slouching down in her seat as the kid kicks again. The one sweater she has with her is already on, and does nothing to lessen the cold catapaulting at her skin. "Do they not have a concept of heating systems? America's using up unsustainable resources, anyway, might as well use it on something useful. God's sakes." When she asks for a blanket from the attendant, passing by, the attendant very politely tell Arizona that they are all out of blankets. Arizona is very, scarily close to flipping her shits.

Jacob stares at her for a second before groaning and pulling his zip-up hoodie off. He flips it over and around, so that it rests half on him, half on her. It's warm, and Arizona holds herself back from sniffing it. She almost cooes at his chivalrous act. Still, she smirks, trying her best not to give away her screaming insides, "Not willing to give all of it up?"

"Ungrateful," he sniffs, and laughing quietly, Arizona scoots closer so that their arms press up against each other, from shoulder to elbow. He is warm and steady. She rustles around in her pocket before pulling out her phone and headphones, and tuckes one of the buds into her left ear. A few pulsed minutes later, Jacob turns his head to glance down at her, at the one earbud in her ear. "What are you listning to?"

"Christmas music."

"For real?"

"Uh, yeah? Christmas is only my favorite holiday, ever."

Silently, Jacob plucks the other headphone from her lap and places it in his right ear. His eyebrows rise.

"Christmas music."

"Yes, Jacob, that is what I sad."

Three songs in, Arizona's eyelids grow heavier. Four songs in, they shut. Five songs in, her head tilts to rest on something that is warm and smells nice, and six songs in, Arizona is asleep. She doesn't even wake for the peanuts and drinks.

"We are fifteen minutes away from landing."

Blinking away her sleep, Arizona squints at the sunlit airplane, at the purple and blue seat in front of her. Turning her head slightly, she finds her head on Jacob's shoulder, and her eyes widen momentarily. Jacob doesn't notice, he is staring out of the window, Arizona's white earbud now laying on his leg. She takes a moment to appreciate his profile, his jawline, before pulling back abruptly. There is a crick in her neck, and when she twists in her seat, about a bajillion muscles crack.

"Sleep well?" asks Jacob, tired, yet amused. Always amused.

"Very." Arizona looks down and finds the sweatshirt totally on her torso, now, but Jacob doesn't seem very cold in his grey waffle shirt. "Thanks for the sweater," she clears her throat, pulling it off and giving it back to him. "And for, um, the shoulder. It's a nice shoulder." She pats the shoulder awkwardly, and Jacob bites back a smile.

"Are you still cold? You can keep my sweatshirt for now, if you like," he says, and blushing a beet red, Arizona shakes her head and looks down.

"No, that's okay. Thanks, though."

"Sure?"

"Yes, Jacob."

"O-kay, just asking. Jeez."

They get off the plane at 11:15. The PDX airport is familiar, and there is this low undertone of constant conversations, everywhere she goes, with families seeing each other again, with blinding grins on their faces. Arizona would just be taking a cab home, because her parents had left to pick up Lara and Ross form the train station and hour before her flight landed. The couple lives only a state up down, in California, so they come to visit via train, which is cheaper, and prettier, apparently.

After baggage claim, Arizona stands outside next to Jacob, waiting for a taxi, and Jacob for his ride. Five minutes of idle talk later, a familiar, blue Toyota pulls up, and Arizona swallows. The car parks right at the curb in front of the two, and the passenger's side's window rolls down to reveal Jeremy leaning over the cupholders with a huge, gorgeous grin.

"Hey, man," Jacob smiles and Jeremy nods.

"How was the flight?"

"Alright. Is the trunk open?"

Jeremy nods and Jacob walks around to put his bags in the back of the car. Arizona stands awkwardly, right hand holding left elbow.

"I, um. I...hi."

"Hey, Arizona. How are you?"

"I'm good! Great, actually. You?"

"I'm alright, yeah." There's an awkward stillness between them as Jacob obliviously walks through and sits down in the shotgun seat. "Do you have a ride?"

"What? Oh, yeah—yeah, I'll just get a taxi." Arizona flails her hand around and Jeremy looks unimpressed.

"Get in. I'll drive you home."

"Oh, no, that's totally fine." Arizona is stumbling for words because ex-boyfriends should never ever be kind to ex-girlfriends like her. Jacob smiles at her expectantly and she nearly falls apart.

"C'mon," says Jeremy kindly. Maybe this would be good for them, their friendship. Step one to renewing lack of awkward is not being awkward.

Finally, she nods hesitantly and takes a deep breath, before tossing her suitcase in the trunk, slamming it shut. Arizona slides into the backseat, and the car smells exactly like it did a year ago: like Jeremy and coffee and like the scent of the air freshener hanging from the rearview mirror in the shape of a blue maple leaf. She can feel the guilt rising up to choke her, and she coughs it away.

The car is silent on the ride home, except for The Strokes in the CD player, but Jacob looks totally at ease, which isn't much of a surprise. Jeremy seems a bit tense, and Arizona may pee her pants.

"So—"

"I—"

She squeezes her eyes shut in embarrassment, and Jeremy chuckles almost sheepishly.

"You go first," his brown eyes meet Arizona's in the mirror. She smiles.

"Just, how is OSU?"

Jeremy had gotten a full ride to Oregon State University, but he had still been staying in dorms, being a freshman and all. Arizona was jealous about the full ride part, but not about the housing situation—she would so rather be in New York than Oregon for undergrad.

"It's great, yeah. My roommate was actually kind of an asshole, but most of the people there are cool."

"Cool, cool..."

Arizona wants to die right now. She should have just taking that stupid taxi, dammit.

"How's NYU? Jacob said it's going good for him."

"Super fun, yeah."

Her house couldn't have appeared soon enough. The inside is dark, and the car that is usually parked in the driveway is gone. "Awesome," she mumbles, stumbling out of the car and pulling her bag from the trunk. Jacob had gotten out of the car to help, but she'd waved him away. She is totally done with cute boys right now. They're the worst. And the best, but mostly the worst, with their freaking charming everythings. Arizona rolls her suitcase up before making a pitstop in front of Jeremy's gaping window. She leans down a little to see him. "Thanks so much for the ride, I really do appreciate it."

"Of course," he smiles warmly and Arizona wants to scream at just how nice Jeremy Miller is. Why, why couldn't he have been some horrible, gross, asshole-of-a-boyfriend, so she wouldn't have felt bad about every stupid thing she did? Why?

Sighing, she leans back up and waves at the two boys before stepping into her house. Just like bucket of ideas about what to do with Jacob, it's empty.

25

— • —

CHAPTER 25

Christmas day, Arizona falls off her bed. It's seven a.m., and her duvet is all tangled up with her legs. Groaning, she lifts her torso off the ground before crawling out of the sheets and leaning her head against the footpost of her bed. It's too early to be doing anything productive.

Pulling on her socks, she takes a breath before heaving herself up and off the ground, and yanking the bedroom door open. Arizona brushes her teeth with blurry eyes, toothpaste dribbling down her chin, and she combs her hair with a series of impatient noises when the teeth of the brush gets stuck in her many blonde tangles.

By the time she makes it up the stairs and onto the main floor, Arizona is awake. She can smell coffee as she nears the kitchen, and she can hear multiple voices speaking at the same time. It feels like Christmas, and Arizona smiles to herself. When she steps onto the linoleum tiles, her mom squeals and hurries to hug her. "Merry Christmas!" Her dad smiles at her and mumbles the same. "We're waiting for you to open the presents."

"How long have you been up?" Arizona raises her brows and Lara sets her coffee mug down.

"Since six."

"Why."

Nobody says anything.

"Where's Ross?"

Lara jerks a thumb behind her, at the living room. Arizona cranes her neck and catches a glimpse of Ross splayed out on one of the couches, arms spread out around him, mouth slightly agape, the tiniest of snores escaping him. Arizona bites back a grin. When Lara yells for him to wake up, he jerks open and sits straight up on the couch, blinking rapidly.

Arizona sits down at the table after filling a cup with tea. There are cookies on the counter, next to a bag of bagels, and Arizona takes one of each, spreading some cream cheese on the bagel. She bites into it, and watches her mother gather up the presents to set on the table before them. Ross joins the family a second later. "Lara...Ross...Arizona...ooh, me! Ben." Arizona had left the presents down in her room, and she sighs sitting back in the chair. She'll get them later, once everybody else is done. Arizona slowly unsticks the pieces of tape pressing down on the carefully wrapped, small box. As soon as she gets it unwrapped, Cora takes the paper, because she's always been a huge believer in the three R's.

Inside is a red, velvet box, and Arizona flips the top open slowly to find a golden charm bracelet inside. "Oh, that's really pretty! Thanks, Mom."

"Dad tacked his name onto that, too," winks Cora and Arizona smiles.

"Thanks, Dad."

Ben nods. The unwrapping of presents proceeds. Lara got Arizona a book she's never heard of before, and Ross got her a Powell's Bookstore gift card. Arizona had brought her presents up from her room. A necklace and earrings set for Lara, a gift card to a furniture store for Cora, glossy photo paper for Ben, and an iTunes card for Ross. Twenty minutes later, the family sits at the kitchen table, mugs of tea spread out before them.

"So," says Arizona's mother, "I haven't seen Jeremy in a while."

Arizona had forgotten to tell everybody about the break-up. Four months ago. Shit.

"We broke up," she tries to say nonchalantly, sipping at her green tea.

"What?"

Cora blinks. Lara freezes. Ross raises his eyebrows. Ben looks totally indifferent.

"Oh, did I forget to tell you guys?"

Nobody says anything, until, "Dammit," hisses Lara, and Arizona looks at her. "I sent his family an invitation."

"To what?"

"To my wedding, Arizona."

"Oh. Well, I'm still friends with him, so it's fine, I guess."

A second passes.

"How'd you guys break up, anyway? And why are you so fine with it?" Cora asks, face concerned, as if Arizona might actually just be hiding all her self-pity and sadness and anger behind a ten-foot-thick wall of bricks that she built to protect herself from the big, bad world. Arizona likes to think that her life isn't half as dramatic as that sounds in her head.

"It was a mutual uncoupling," she nods, pronouncing uncoupling in distinct syllables.

"He didn't dump you, then?" asks Lara, and Arizona shakes her head. "Huh."

Arizona stares.

"What does that mean?"

Lara shrugs and gets up, walking out of the kitchen, mug in hand.

There's an invitation on her desk. It is cream colored with silver accenting on the border, and the writing is in royal purple. Embossed at the top, it says:

Lara May and Ross Williams

Then:

Come celebrate with us!

February 14, 2016

Beneath that, it states the time and place, and then at the bottom, there are two boxes, one to check if the guest is bringing a date, and the other for if the guest is coming alone. The paper feels rough under her fingers, and it smells strongly of ink and paper, as if completely fresh off a printer somewhere.

Picking it up delicately, for that is how the piece of paper demands to be held, Arizona skips every other step running up the stairs to the living room. Lara is lounging on the sofa, flipping through a glossy magazine with freshly-painted, teal nails. She looks up as soon as she hears Arizona, and a pretty smile blooms on her lips. "Isn't it beautiful?" she asks with wide eyes, and Arizona nods.

"Do I have to bring a date?"

"Nope, but I actually have my own question for you."

"Okay."

Lara gestures for Arizona to sit, but she shakes her head and leans against a chair, instead. Lara shrugs.

"'Kay. So. Do you want to be a bridesmaid?"

"Am I not Maid of Honor?" Arizona sks, completely joking. Lara blanches, very distinct compared to her usually perfectly tan skin tone. She looks at Arizona with a startled expression.

"I, uh, I asked Kiera. I just—I thought you wouldn't care either way." Arizona is revelling in hearing her sister totally uncomfortable. And Arizona feels only a little bit guilty. "Because, I mean, if you hadn't noticed, we're not the closest of sisters, and she's my—"

"Kidding, Lara."

"Oh, thank fuck."

"What?"

"God. Thank God."

"Right."

"So?"

"What?"

"Bridesmaid?"

Arizona smiles a small, fleeting smile before nodding. "Yeah, I'd love to."

The Mays always keep their door unlocked on Christmas Day. Arizona never knows why, seeing as Christmas Day doesn't necessarily mean Safe Day. Then again, there is only so much danger in the suburbs of some relatively small, west coast city.

Neighbors and family usually filter in through the unlocked door throughout the day. Alex arrives at half-past noon, a red wagon in tow. It gets stuck in doorways multiple times, and hits many things, and Arizona watches in amusement from the kitchen as he makes his way down the hallway. A second later, Chris, the always-tired boyfriend, opens the door again and follows after, shaking his head. He rolls his eyes as Alex nearly trips over the kitchen door's threshold, before placing his hand gently on Alex's back to help him into the kitchen, and then onto a couch in the connecting living room.

Alex lets the handle of the wagon fall to the carpeted ground, and Arizona can now see several presents in it. "Arizona!" He grins and grabs her in a huge hug before situating her back onto the bar stool, and then tips an imaginary hat charmingly at Lara, who smiles and slides off her chair to hug him delicately.

"Hey," says Chris, weary smile on. Arizona grins at him. He's never really been the touchy-feely kind. "Merry Christmas, you guys."

Alex cuts the girls off before they can say anything. Arizona wonders how her parents can't hear him from upstairs, and how they haven't come downstairs to see who it is. "So, as you guys may know..." he ambles towards the wagon and turns to face them, hands situated on either side of his hips, "...it's Christmas. And I have presents." Practically splitting his face with another beaming smile, he grabs two wrapped boxes and hands them to Arizona and Lara.

"Oh, wow, you shouldn't have," Lara says with her sultry voice, and Alex waves her away.

"Shut up and open the present, Lara."

"Okay."

Arizona slides a finger under the tape, and pulls on the paper, watching it come apart in her lap. Amongst the shiny wrapping paper is a box, and in the box is a turntable.

"Holy shit."

"I decided that it was time to make you a hipster, too."

"I don't have any records, Alex?"

"Ah."

He raises a finger, telling her to wait for it, before turning back around with a thin bag. Arizona slides out two, old vinyls. Bob Marley and The Police.

"Holy shit," she repeats. Beside her, her older sister is holding a big book, square in shape, covered with a black, pleather cover. It's of some dancer Lara basically worships, and she's laughing in wonderment.

"Thanks so much!"

"There's only so much an almost-dad could do," he waves them away. "Also, you're getting married, I heard?"

"Oh, yeah, it's whatever," grins Lara and he nods.

"I'd say."

Thursday, January 1

Six days after Christmas, Arizona walks to The Number. Briana and Romy had been on vacation over Christmas week, so everybody had just decided to meet up once the two get back. They're back, and Crosley had decided that it'd be great to meet up at the Millers' restaurant.

"Yeah, man, get us discounts and shit," he'd shrugged when Arizona had asked him "The Number as in my ex's restaurant?"

Arizona unwinds her red scarf from around her throat as she yanks open the heavy doors. Inside it is warm, and smells of cinnamon and chocolate. Arizona's actually really missed the place, and she sighs, walking to the table all the way at the corner, where she spots the oh-so-familiar dark brown head. Wiping away a smile, she makes sure to sit down across from him with a deadpan expression.

"Hey," he nods at her. They sit there in silence for a second before laughing and getting up for a hug. "How've you been?"

"Who are you, and what have you done to Crosley."

"What does that mean?"

"Uh, you never ask stuff about how people have been, are you sick?" Arizona reaches over to place the back of her hand on his forehead, only half joking. "Do you have a fever? You're pretty warm."

"Hot, Arizona, I'm hot."

"Someone needs to shut you up," Arizona rolls her eyes. He grins. "Preferably Gem. Preferably, preferably with a kiss." The grin drops.

"Go to hell."

"I'll meet you there."

"Yes, let's carpool."

"No, but seriously, Cros. When are you going to ask her out?" The boy doesn't say anything, he just looks at her, tracing a line running down the wooden table repeatedly. Arizona squints at him before reclining in her seat, mouth dropping open. "Oh, my God. Crosley, have you already asked her out?" He still stays silent. "Holy fucking shit. I—"

"Crosley, what have you done now." Romy slumps down next to Arizona with a roll of her eyes. Arizona grins, in what she imagines an evil manner in her head, as she turns to the other girl. Arizona totally ignores Crosley's multiple kicks of warning under the table, as she tells Romy exactly what Crosley's done now.

Once the other two girls arrive, a boy Arizona knows much too well comes over to the table, black apron tied around his waist. "Jeremy."

"Hey, Arizona."

"I..."

"How are you?"

"Good, thanks. You?"

"Great."

"Awesome."

Briana clears her throat.

"So, uh, what can I get you guys?"

The five rattle off their order and with a short nod and smile, Jeremy turns around to walk back to the kitchen.

"Well," Briana clears her throat, "we now know who had sex with who."

"Jhyeah," snorts Romy, "Crosley and Gem."

Gem twists Romy's ear and Crosley gets up, threatening to leave, and doesn't sit back down until Briana calms him down, smile bitten down nonetheless.

"Put your blinker on. Put your—goddammit, Arizona, but your blinker on!" Crosley scowls and falls back into the passenger's seat as a car zooms past, honking. He runs a hand throug his hair exhasperatedly, leaning his elbow on the side of the car. Arizona frowns,

"You know I don't respond well to orders under pressure!"

"Well, you're going to have to!"

"You're mean, Crosley. College has made you mean," Arizona glares, and he rolls his eyes.

"You're annoying and a terrible student."

Arizona knows he's only irritated right now because she had brought up Gem before the lesson. she had pointed out that Crosley still hadn't kissed her, and if he didn't grow a pair and do it soon, someone else would and he would never get to kiss Gem's face off. Crosley had told her that he wouldn't talk about this, but she'd prodded, until he'd eventually said that he wouldn't teach her jackshit if she didn't shut the fuck up.

"Thanks, I appreciate it."

"Oh, that's great! Then I guess you'd appreciate me socking you in the mouth even more!"

Arizona clicks her tongue.

"Sticks and stones, Crosley. Also, hasn't your mother taught you that hitting doesn't solve any problems, long-term?"

"I don't care about long-term at the moment," he mutters. Arizona stares at him for a second before flicking two fingers at his cheek. "Jesus, Arizona, watch the road!"

"I was showing affection."

"Gross."

"Cute."

"Thanks."

"Oh—no, did I not make it clear? Gem. She's cute. Very cute, don't you agree, Cros?"

"Stop the car, I'm getting out."

Arizona keeps driving and locks the door. Crosley slams against the passenger side's window dramatically, catching the attention of a middle-aged woman in the car beside them. She looks at him with a panicked expression, and Crosley finally eases up, laughing.

Arizona punches his arm really hard. He yelps, and she grins. "I love you, Crosley."

"Whatever."

"Say it back. Say you love me."

"No."

"Say it back, Crosley."

"Fuck you."

"Thank you. Now that wasn't so hard, was it?"

"What?"

Cleaning out her room is difficult as it is, and it just gets even worse when Arizona finds Jeremy's things throughout it. It just means that she'll have to return them. After two hours, her room is sufficiently neat, and there is a plastic bag on her bed, filled with things that don't belong to her.

A small notebook from a science project long ago; a thumb drive in the shape of a skateboard; tangled, black earbuds;a black scarf she'd borrowed when she walked back from his house one cold afternoon. Arizona has no idea how so many things of his had been left in her room.

Deciding that it's better to be done and over with it, Arizona gathers up everything in the bag and shrugs on a sweatshirt. Grabbing the keys on the way out, she yells to her mother that she's going out. She's gone before Cora can ask where. The drive to Jeremy's house is five minutes, much too short for her taste. She only gets through one and a half songs on the radio.

It's three o'clock in the afternoon. The sun is out, but the air is cold, and Arizona rocks back and forth on her feet as she waits for someone to answer the door. It's been two minutes since she'd rang the bell for the second time, and Arizona shrugs, turning back towards the car. Oh, well, at least she tried. Arizona nearly curses when a blue sedan pulls up to the curb.

Instead of the boy she'd been expecting to step out, the other brother does, and Arizona wonders if she can pull out of the driveway without him spotting her. Jacob doesn't see her until he locks the car and looks up.

"Hey," he says.

Arizona hops off the step to smile at Jacob, who throws her his beautiful grin to fumble with. His hair is mussed up in a way only a lot of work can do—Arizona's seen it many times at The Numbers during afterhours—and his eyes are puffy from sleep deprivation. "You okay?"

"Oh, yeah. We actually catered for a wedding today. The rest of the family's still there, but I finished cooking and preparing, so I came back. were you looking for someone?" he asks, walking past her to unlock the door. Jacob leaves the door wide open for her as he disappears into the house, and Arizona enters a second later, following him a bit uncertainly.

"Jeremy, actually." She can't see his face, but he nods casually, throwing his keys into the dish by the home phone. "I, uh, have...some of his stuff. that he left at my place. when..." she trails off, shrugging, and Jacob yanks the fridge open, pulling out a little tupper-ware box of pasta. He flips the cap off and sniffs at it before shrugging and placing it in the microwave, setting it to a minute.

"You want any?" he asks and she shakes her head. Jacob turns around to lean against a counter, legs crossed at the ankle, fork in his fingers tapping against his lips, as he studies her with great blue eyes. "What did he leave?" he asks as idle conversation.

"Just...stuff. You know, like a notebok and earbuds, and stuff." Arizona doesn't bother fishing them out from her bag. Jacob nods, humming a barely familiar tune under his breath.

"How serious were you guys?" he asks mindlessly. He stretches his arms above his head and his white button-down stretches ridiculously well around his muscles. Clearing her throat, arizona looks away, inwardly cursing at herself.

"Okay serious? I guess? God, I don't know. Now that I think about it, nothing in our relationship was really sure, y'know?" Arizona blinks, pursing her lips, and Jacob snorts, just a little bit.

"Yeah, I definitely know."

He cranes his neck to peek at the microwave.

"You know that you still work at The Number, right?"

"Oh—yeah, I mean, well, Jeremy said I can, but...I just feel like it would be awkward."

He nods and purses his lips.

"Jacob."

"Hm."

"We're friends, yeah?"

He stares at her for a second before blinking, shaking his head just a little, and looking away. He smiles.

"Yeah."

"Oh."

His eyes snap up to hers again. "What?"

"What what?"

"What was that oh. Why'd you sound so disappointed?"

His eyes narrow at her and arizona stutters, opening and shutting her mouth, unsure what exactly to say at this point. "I didn't...?" Jacob smiles at her with this half-amused-half-tired smile. The microwave beeps four times but he doesn't kick off the counter to get his pasta. Arizona blinks. "Your pasta's r—"

"Arizona May, do you like me?"

Arizona chokes. Jacob waits patiently for her breath, as he's done so many times before.

"What?"

Jacob doesn't bother repeating himself. He never does repeat himself when it comes to Arizona, because he knows she's always listening to everything he says, that smug little fucker. He tilts his head to the side, this concentrated looks on his face.

"I mean," he continues with a shrug, "I wouldn't blame you. I just realized how much I flirt with you." Arizona's eyes get larger, and he finally straightens up, but instead of going to the microwave, he takes a step towards her. Two steps. "I don't even realize that I'm doing it, sometimes."

Sometimes.

"I tend to do that with girls I like."

What the fuck is going on?

Three steps.

They are four inches apart.

Arizona can't breathe.

Arizona doesn't know what she's supposed to say. Ahe doesn't know what she can say. But that's okay, because then, Jacob leans down, erases all the inches between their faces, and kisses her.

26

EPILOGUE

Arizona has decided that she likes weddings only when she is not important to them.

"Lara, calm down."

"Don't tell me to calm down! What if Ross says the wrong name up there, or something!"

"What ever gave you that idea," Arizona says blandly, falling into a chair.

"I can't breathe, oh, my God."

Sighing, Arizona stretches forward to hand her sister a water bottle, and Lara takes it, chugging down half of it immediately. Her other hand rises to fan herself at an increasingly terrifyingly rapid pace, and after two more seconds, Arizona curls her fingers around her older sister's delicate wrist to place it back down in her lap gently.

"I'll be right back. Do you think you'll be alright?" Arizona says, even though of course Lara won't be alright. Lara doesn't respond, and after ordering her to try snake breathing, Arizona leaves the room. She can't believe that she was kind of excited for this when she woke up that morning.

As she steps into the hallway, a man hurries past, a cardboard box barely in his arms. Nearly falling over, Arizona throws and arm out, just catching herself by bracing against the doorjamb. With a loud sigh, she continues downstairs. In the kitchen she finds Kiera touching up on the cake. Lara's best friend and maid of honor just so happens to be an amazing cook, and has her own catering company, so not only had she helped out with all the wedding planning, she had also cooked for the entire thing, as well. Arizona can only begin to imagine just how much Kiera's life resembles hell at the moment.

"Kiera, I can't calm her down."

"Shit," the girl in mention hisses, flicking a perfect, black ringlet away from her face and jabs at a spot on the cake with a frosting cone. "Shitshitshitshitshit." Arizona purses her lips for a second.

"K—"

"Fuck."

"O-kay," Arizona mumbles, turning around to head out of the kitchen.

"Arizona?" She swivels on her heels to face Kiera again, who is now looking at her.

"That's me."

"Did you need something?"

"Oh—oh, yeah, uh, Lara's kind of having a melt-down and I apparently can't do anything about it, and not even complimenting her look today is helping and I have no idea what to do."

"Lovely," Kiera says with a slight smile before patting Arizona on the shoulder on the way out. Arizona doesn't know how she does it. Only the nicest person ever could manage to keep Lara as their best friend. Shaking her head, Arizona strolls into the kitchen to peer at the cake. It's beautiful, tall, and a pastel yellow, covered in candied flowers. Holding herself back from reaching out to swipe a finger at it, she shakes her head and turns, only to nearly run into someone.

"Oh, sorry," she mumbles, stepping back a few, to peer up at Jacob. He's holding a tray above her head, with a startled expression, and Arizona's cheeks flush with total betrayal.

"J—Jacob. Hi. Uh, are you..."

"Yeah, we're catering. Everything but the cake." He looks behind her. "That's a very pretty cake," his brows rise, "did you buy it?"

"Erm, no, Lara's best friend made it. Kiera? I don't know if you know her."

"Nope, guess I'll meet her later."

"Guess so." They stand awkwardly, until he clears his throat, and Arizona remembers the tray of rolls in his hands. "Oh! Sorry." She shuffles out of the way, and with a hint of a smile, he sets it down on the counter.

"You alright?" he turns around to lean against the counter in a familiar gesture, smiling with something Arizona doesn't recognize.

"Fine. Totally fine."

Jacob's teasing her, she can tell. She wouldn't blame him, after what happened the last time they saw each other.

"Arizona May, do you like me?"

Arizona chokes. Jacob waits patiently for her breath, as he's done so many times before.

"What?"

Jacob doesn't bother repeating himself. He never does repeat himself when it comes to Arizona, because he knows she's always listening to everything he says, that smug little fucker. He tilts his head to the side, this concentrated looks on his face.

"I mean," he continues with a shrug, "I wouldn't blame you. I just realized how much I flirt with you." Arizona's eyes get larger, and he finally straightens up, but instead of going to the microwave, he takes a step towards her. Two steps. "I don't even realize that I'm doing it, sometimes."

Sometimes.

"I tend to do that with girls I like."

What the fuck is going on?

Three steps.

They are four inches apart.

Arizona can't breathe.

Arizona doesn't know what she's supposed to say. She doesn't know what she can say. But that's okay, because then, Jacob leans down, erases all the inches between their faces, and kisses her. She sighs against his lips and molds against him pathetically quickly, and his smile melts through their mouths. He pulls away first, and the rush of cold is immediate, and big.

She bites her lip and stares at him for a couple seconds before shaking her head. Jacob looks at her, face half-amusement, half-questioning. Arizona doesn't know what to do, she doesn't know what she can do, what's acceptable, and what's not, anymore, so she just leans up, kisses him once more, long and hard, before pulling back just as fast and almost running out the door. His confusion is tangible in the air following her, and Arizona wants to scream and smile and laugh until she cries all at the same time and shit. Shitshitshitshitshit. Her heart is beating a mile a minute, which is insane in and of itself, seeing as it doesn't feel like she's even breathing, much less alive, and Arizona forces herself to get in her car and drive, when all she wants to do is fall onto his yard and make snow angels. Jesus, someone needs to shove a snowball down her jacket.

"You cut your hair."

Arizona blinks.

Her hand reaches up instinctively to touch her now-chin-length hair. "Oh—yeah. It was getting really long and heavy, and I thought I'd cut it, and that it'll be nice for the wedding, so—" she cuts herself off before she says she will regret but not be able to swallow back.

"I like it. You look very pretty."

"Oh."

"I..." Jacob scratches his head, and his hair messes up in the way Arizona loves, "I need to get some more stuff from the car and help set up and stuff so...I'll see you tonight, okay?"

"Oh! Oh, yeah, sure I'll get out of your way. Sorry. See you," she laughs breathily for no reason whatsoever. Arizona wants someone to kick her. With a smile, Jacob nods and leaves the kitchen, and Arizona is alone again, which allows enough time for her to mentally punch herself.

The venue is a pretty courtyard behind a small, quaint, brick cottage with ivy crawling up and down every side. It's like the ones Arizona's seen on television and online, because, obviously, Lara would settle for no less. If she has a wedding Pinterest, then she will have a Pinterest wedding.

At the moment, Arizona is very scarily balanced on a ladder, trying to get some white fairy lights strung up. As adorable as they are, they are just as irritating. The wire is either too twisty or not twisty enough, and just as she's about to give up, someone asks her if she's alright up there. Rolling her eyes a little, she glances down, and sees a very blonde boy with a charming grin she can tell has loosened many girls' pants before.

"Uhhh..." she blinks, because she has never seen him before, "I will be, I guess. I just need to figure out how to string these little shits, because they won't stay, and also I'm not the biggest fan of ladders." The boy looks up at the rods she's supposed to wind the strings around for a few more seconds, before gesturing for her to climb down. With a sigh, Arizona does, and he takes a hold of the lights in her hand before climbing up the steps she just jumped off. She watches as he tries to situate the lights. Despite it being a fairly cold winter, today's forecast is hopefully sunny. It's one in the afternoon, and the sun is very apparent, but the chill is still there.

Arizona rubs her arms and bites the inside of her lip. "Who are you?"

He pauses, with his hands still up, and looks at her. "I'm Dane." She blinks.

"Who are you?" she repeats, and he laughs.

"I'm Ross' brother."

"Oh. Okay."

She can see the resemblance now, not just in the hair, but also in the eyes, and the grin.

"You're Lara's sister, right? Arizona?"

"That's me."

"Sweet."

Arizona nods a bit awkwardly, and after a minute, he starts climbing back down.

"It's all good for now. Should we test it?" She nods, and he plugs it in, and immediately every single light starts glowing, but she can't tell if it's pretty or not, because it's still in broad daylight. With a shrug, Dane unplugs it. "Huh, guess we have to wait and see then."

"I guess so. Thanks for the help."

"Sure. Just helping a sister out," he grins, elbowing her gently, and Arizona rolls her eyes again, but she's smiling a little too. And then she realizes that she's going to have two brothers the next day. Totally weird. "I'll catch you later, yeah? I think my date's arriving soon, because she wants to help and stuff."

"Sure, see you."

When Arizona turns she catches a glimpse of dark hair, and she knows that particular shade could only belong to a certain family, so she decides to book it.

Lara looks even prettier than usual, which Arizona hadn't even known was possible. But she does, and that's kind of crazy. It had taken Kiera forty-five minutes to sort her out, but it had happened eventually, and now Lara is back to being totally composed, totally gorgeous, and totally ready to handle anything and everything, as long as it doesn't involve ripping her dress or ruining her hair.

"You look awesome," Arizona smiles, and Lara frowns at the mirror.

"Really? You think? I feel like something's off."

"What are you talking about, everything is perfect, you look perfect."

The dress falls straight down Lara's body, and it's simple and pretty, not a wedding dress Arizona would have expected from her older sister. The first layer is pearl-colored silk, with a sweetheart neckline, and then on top of that, is a thin layer of white lace, as sleeves and reaching all the way to her collarbone. Lara had been growing out her hair ever since elementary school for this exact day, and Arizona couldn't say that she blames her, because it's holy-shit pretty, in a half-up do, the bottom in loose, soft, and very, very shiny curls. A thin, silver tiara sits right behind her bangs, and Arizona honestly cannot find one flaw in Lara.

"Can you take a picture, please?" Lara asks, "I don't trust the mirror." Repressing another roll of her eyes, Arizona swings the camera around to the front to take a picture. She's designated photographer for the night, Lara decided that they don't need a professional photographer for the actual wedding.

Arizona focuses on Lara, and sighs when she looks through the viewfinder. Lara has her lips pursed, eyebrows furrowed. "Can you at least smile? Just because this is a picture for you to pick all the flaws out of doesn't mean you don't smile." Hesitantly, Lara stretches her lip in the fakest looking smile of all time. "Lara, come on. You know how to smile. Think of something funny, or cute, or happy, I dunno, just smile, dammit." Finally, the older girl pulled one out and it looked half-natural, so Arizona took the shot, and showed her. After a split second, Lara pulls away, shaking her head.

"I knew it, my powder isn't blended well enough. I should fix tha—" She reaches for the brush, and Arizona grabs her wrist gently.

"Lara, your powder is fine, everything is fine. I think you're just freaking out again, and honestly, there's no reason to be, because everything will be fine. I promise."

"You promise?"

"I promise."

"I don't care if you promise, it's human nature to lie, you could very well be lying right now."

"I'm getting Kiera."

"I just don't understand why you always have to wear fuckin' sneakers with everything."

"Oh, sure, when boys on TV wear converse with suits it's cute and he's so adorable, but when Crosley wears it, nooo."

"Please don't refer to yourself in third person, people already think you're stupid."

"No, you think I'm stupid, because you're mean."

Romy rolls her eyes

"Anyway," he says, a bit more softly, "Gem likes it."

At this, Romy actually cracks a grin and shakes her head a lil bit, muttering "whipped" under her breath. Crosley shoves her before sauntering over to where Arizona tries and tries again to organize the drinks table in a "casual, yet sophisticated, yet a little indie" way, as per Lara's requests.

"Watcha doin'," he says.

"Nice shoes," says Arizona.

"Fuck this," sighs Crosley. "Need any help? I don't feel like hanging around Romy right now."

"I do, actually. Could you get those two drink coolers under the table, please? And that fancy thing with the spigot on top, right here."

He snorts, "If you thought I was actually offering, you've got something coming."

"Crosley."

"Just kidding! Just kidding. Jeez, are all women irritable on all wedding days?"

"Dude. Please. Just get the fucking stuff, man." He apologizes quickly and does what he'd been told, and after ten minutes—the duration it had taken him to drag everything over—he leans his hip against the table and looks at her. Arizona frowns at him and he takes his weight off the table quickly, but remains staring. "What?"

"So."

"So?"

"Kissed any Jacobs lately?"

Arizona chokes on air and Crosley patiently waits for it to end, rubbing her back soothingly.

"How did you know?"

"I didn't, actually," he grins cheekily, "until now. That was actually just supposed to be a joke to, like, embarrass you or get you red, or something, but damn. You kissed him? Again?"

"Actually, he kissed me, so."

"Oh, yes!" His hands fly in the air dramatically. "All the difference!"

"Whatever, Crosley. Go make some guyfriends. Talk to Dane, he's nice."

"Rude."

"So, kissed any Gems lately?"

Crosley's flush is immediate and completely apparent, and Arizona's mouth is agape.

"No way. Seriously? How was it? She's a much better kisser than you, isn't she."

"I'm not telling."

"What! No, Cros! Please?"

"You're mean to me, Arizona."

"Cros, I love you."

"No."

Lara and Ross get married three hours later, and Arizona nearly cries.

The sun is setting, and everyone is slowly moving to the other side of the cottage to the dance floor for the reception. She scurries to plug the fairy lights in, and she can actually see them, this time. It's loud, and a little warm, but the sunset is the prettiest thing, every color in the entire world.

After a half hour Lara and Ross are announced to the floor for the first time ever as a married couple, and Lara looks kind of like a fairy in her dress. Ross hasn't stopped grinning the entire night. Arizona sits with her friends at a circular table. She is twisted in her chair because the back is to the floor, and she rests her chin on her hands on the back, watching the couple twirl and dance and move in a way that seems completely impossible.

Crosley and Gem have been close the entire night, always whispering things to each other, always teasing each other in a much more open flirtatious manner, that the other girls find amusement and also disgust in, sometimes. "I'm going to get some water," says Arizona, but nobody acknowledges her, because everyone's mesmerized by the dancing. She shimmies her way around the tables and standing people to the table to find the water container empty. Sighing, she gathers it up, much lighter than expected, and starts to the kitchen in the cottage. It's quite a struggle getting through the doors.

She places the container on the counter, filling it with ice cubes and lemons, and then putting it under the filter, waiting for it to fill with water. Arizona turns and taps the counter with her painted nails, looking around the counter. Food trays lay empty by the sink, some glasses by them. She spots the back door open, and heads over to close it.

It's night by now, and the sky is completely clear, and every star is so bright it might as well be daytime. A chill runs past her, and as she goes to shut the door, she catches glimpse of a shadow sitting on the ground against the wall. Her eyes adjust, and lo and behold, fucking Jacob. His legs are stretched out before him, crossed at the ankles, and he holds a glass in his hand, swirling the contents inside and watching them.

He senses her presence and looks up, a friendly smile immediate. Wordlessly, he spreads his jacket out on the ground next to him, as an invitation, and after a little hesitation, she takes it. She sits with her knees together, pressed against her chest, and her arms wrapped around them.

"Great wedding," he comments after a second.

"It is."

"Your sister and Ross are really in love, huh?"

Arizona nods and then looks at Jacob, and his eyes are already on hers, and they're so blue she might heave. "Fuck," she hisses, but try as she might, she can't not keep looking because they're so blue she might heave.

"What?" he smirks, like he's too lazy to give a full smile, but it's a kind smirk.

"I like you a lot. Fuck!"

"Oh." His eyebrows rise, and this is probably as surprised as she's ever seen him. "Oh, okay, uh. I..."

"But you're Jeremy's brother, and Jeremy is so fucking nice. Like, sometimes I wish he were this complete dick I could hate without even thinking about it, because that would make all of this so much more easier, you know? But he's not, because he's, like, the sweetest human being ever, and goddammit, Jacob." She rests her head on her knees for a second. "I'd love it if you said something right about now." He doesn't, for a few solid minutes.

"Look, Arizona."

"May. Arizona May."

"Look, Arizona May. I like you a lot, too, and sometimes I wish Jeremy were a dick, too. And I wish a lot more than sometimes that we were together and that I'd kissed you more than twice by now and that I'd been to your dorm more than a couple times by now and that I hadn't taken so long to talk to you at school, but I had, and it kind of sucks complete shit. But it's not like either of us can change anything."

"You want to date me?"

"Well, no, I want to be in a relationship with you."

"Oh. God."

"Why do you sound so disgusted, I thought you like me."

"I'm disgusted with myself, because I want to be in a relationship with you, too, but you're Jeremy Miller's fucking brother. I'm the worst person in the world."

"Hey, no you're not. Because since we're basically in the same boat right now, you're not the worst. You're one of the worst!" Arizona smiles, peeking at him from the corner of her eye. "But, look. If you don't remember, you owe me quite a lot of favors. So just do this thing. You don't feel comfortable dating. And I don't want to make you uncomfortable. So we won't date. You and Jeremy split up as friends. I want you to stay friends, you want to stay friends. Stay friends."

Arizona wants to yell at him that she does want to date, though. She wants to be his girlfriend, and she wants to call him her boyfriend, and she wants to go places together, and she wants to kiss him whenever she wants, and she wants to hold his stupid, large hands. But she can't, because he's right, and Arizona needs to heave again.

From the other side of the building she can hear hollers, and knows some uncle must be dancing, and she stands up suddenly.

"I need a drink." She can't look him in the eye, or she knows she'll just collapse again. She knows that he's looking straight at her, though.

"Okay."

When she enters the kitchen, the water container is overflowing, and lemons are floating out. Arizona wants to cry for the second time this night, for completely different reasons.

It takes Arizona quite a while to get the water back, and Jeremy actually shows up after a second, and helps her lug it out. They stand awkwardly by the table, now, watching the floor, where more couples have joined. Arizona sips on water.

"You like him, don't you."

"What?" Arizona frowns at a tiny spill of the water on her dress.

"Jacob. You like him, don't you."

"I..."

"Don't apologize," Jeremy smiles, not unkindly. "We're not together, it's fine."

"But, I am sorry," says Arizona, shaking her head. "I really wish it weren't him of all people, you know? But it is, and maybe if I stay away from him long enough, I'll get over this little crush or whatever it is, but—"

"It's okay. I'm okay with it."

"Really?"

"I mean—no," he fesses, face sheepish. "I mean, it's kind of weird that my ex-girlfriend is dating my brother, you know? But I'll get used to it. I'll get okay."

"Well, I mean, I wouldn't go that far as to say we're dating—"

"Then date him."

"What?" Arizona blinks a couple times, incredibly taken aback.

"Date him. I fucked up so bad when I kissed his fiancé, even when I didn't initiate it, and he obviously likes you, and we broke up on good terms because we never actually liked each other that much, and he may be older than me, but I still don't want to see him get hurt, and wow, I sound really sappy right now, but be nice to him. Please."

"I would never—yeah." Arizona swallows her words, smiling at Jeremy, who grins back. "Yeah, okay." She goes to hug him but he tenses up visibly, taking a step back.

"Don't hug me, Arizona."

Arizona is frozen, arms still raised, and Jeremy laughs.

"Just kidding." He enters her embrace, and Arizona pinches him lightly, and he yelps.

"Whatever, Jeremy."

Arizona's mom stumbles towards them, looking the slightest bit more than a little tipsy. "Arizona, honey! Having a good time? You did a great job setting everything up." Her eyes focus on Jeremy and brighten visibly. "Oh, you must be a Miller!"

Jeremy grins, nodding.

"Jeremy's younger brother, then?"

"Uh—no, I am Jeremy," he laughs a little, and Arizona is horrified, and wishes that she were anywhere else at the moment.

"No, you're silly is what you are," laughs Mrs. May. "I met Jeremy a number of times! He's taller and has different eyebrows. Also, I don't know for sure, but I'm pret-ty sure that he has blu-u-ue eyes."

"She's so drunk," Arizona laughs breathily and Jeremy smiles. Her mom frowns at her.

"I am not that drunk! I can still tell who's who, and he is not Jeremy."

"Okay, well, I'd love to stay and chat," says Jeremy, with pursed lips, "but I actually need to go check on the food. So, see you around?"

"Sure, yeah. See you...around," Arizona waves a bit awkwardly, and he nods at her one more time, in a way that says "tell him now, please,"

"What was he talking about, being Jeremy?" Cora asks with her head tilted.

"Nothing. He wasn't saying anything."

"What?"

"Look, he's Jeremy, and the boy you thought was Jeremy was actually Jacob, the older brother, and I wasn't actually dating Jacob, I was taking Jeremy, the boy you just met, but he was never able to make it to the dinner to meet you, but Lara was being totally irritating, so I told you that Jacob was Jeremy, and then he just pretended to be Jeremy from then on, because he's just a really good guy! Oh, my God," mutters Arizona, mostly to herself, "he's such a good guy. I like him so much."

She turns and walks away, her mom completely confused behind her. But Cora's a little drunk, so she shrugs. Jacob isn't where she saw him last, and with a sigh, she hunts for him for what seems like hours, before she spots him by a tree in the back, also watching the dancing. She approaches him slowly, cautiously, and he doesn't notice her until she calls his name softly. He turns and smiles at her.

"Arizona May."

"Yeah."

"Did you dance yet?"

She ignores this.

"I talked to Jeremy."

Jacob stays silent, waiting.

"And honestly, I appreciate that you're saying to not date, because I do care about my relationship with Jeremy, but I also care about my relationship with you, and I talked to Jeremy, and he says that I should basically just be honest with you, but I already did that before I talked to him, so I'm here just to lay it down flat, again. I like you, Jacob. I think you're great, and also kind of hot, and I want to be your girlfriend. And that's it. So."

He doesn't say anything for the longest while, and Arizona considers telling him to think about it, while she goes to the bathroom, because she might have had too much water. Jacob isn't looking at her, he's playing with the cup still in his hands. When he turns to her, his face is the scariest thing in the world because there is no expression, and there has never been a time in the portion of Arizona's life that she's known the Millers that she hasn't been able to tell what he's thinking. He opens his mouth, then shuts it.

"You talked to him?"

Arizona nods.

"And he says this is okay? Genuinely?"

She nods, again.

"He actually explicitly told me to date you, so," she laughs a little nervously, almost, and shrugs, "look how that turned out!"

"You want to date me?"

"God, yes."

Jacob kisses her.

Hard.

www.ingramcontent.com/pod-product-compliance
Lightning Source LLC
Chambersburg PA
CBHW070923190726
48292CB00004B/1079